Such Fine Boys

ENGLISH TRANSLATIONS OF WORKS BY PATRICK MODIANO

From Yale University Press
After the Circus
Little Jewel
Paris Nocturne
Pedigree: A Memoir
Such Fine Boys
Sundays in August
Suspended Sentences: Three Novellas (Afterimage, Suspended Sentences, and *Flowers of Ruin)*

Also available or forthcoming
The Black Notebook
Catherine Certitude
Dora Bruder
Honeymoon
In the Café of Lost Youth
Lacombe Lucien
Missing Person
Out of the Dark
So You Don't Get Lost in the Neighborhood
The Occupation Trilogy (The Night Watch, Ring Roads, and *La Place de l'Etoile)*
A Trace of Malice
Villa Triste
Young Once

Such Fine Boys

PATRICK MODIANO

TRANSLATED FROM THE FRENCH BY MARK POLIZZOTTI

WITH A FOREWORD BY J. M. G. LE CLÉZIO

YALE UNIVERSITY PRESS ■ NEW HAVEN & LONDON

A MARGELLOS
WORLD REPUBLIC OF LETTERS BOOK

The translator would like to thank Rebecca Thompson for her excellent suggestions.

The Margellos World Republic of Letters is dedicated to making literary works from around the globe available in English through translation. It brings to the English-speaking world the work of leading poets, novelists, essayists, philosophers, and playwrights from Europe, Latin America, Africa, Asia, and the Middle East to stimulate international discourse and creative exchange.

Yale University Press books may be purchased in quantity for educational, business, or promotional use. For information, please e-mail sales.press@yale.edu (U.S. office) or sales@yaleup.co.uk (U.K. office).

Set in Electra and Nobel types by Tseng Information Systems, Inc.
Printed in the United States of America.

Library of Congress Control Number: 2016962442
ISBN 978-0-300-22334-7 (paperback : alk. paper)

A catalogue record for this book is available from the British Library.

This paper meets the requirements of ANSI/NISO z39.48-1992
(Permanence of Paper).

10 9 8 7 6 5 4 3 2 1

FOR RUDY
FOR SIMONE

. . . Such a fine boy!

—Turgenev, "Bezhin Meadow"

CONTENTS

Over the past three decades, Patrick Modiano has built a body of work on the most consequential of themes: the theme of memory, of the ghosts that circulate through the postwar world and among its survivors.

He does not approach this theme with a polemicist's plume or avenger's sword. Rather, he treats it like a research component or analytical tool, rendering it via allusions, enigmas, measured accents. He does not offer up heroes or advance toward a goal. He proceeds by questions rather than affirmations.

In this tightly woven ensemble—for Modiano's writings never succumb to facility or digression, never stray from the line he established as of his first volume, *La Place de l'Etoile* (leaving aside his slight deviation into film with *Lacombe Lucien*)—*Such Fine Boys* occupies a place apart, first by its structure, a suite of brief narratives, like interconnected short stories; then by its implicit reference to the author's personal experience.

Of all Modiano's novels, this is at once the clearest, the purest, and the most complex. Each of his major themes appears in it, linking this book with both his previous volumes and those that followed. This is my favorite of Modiano's works, because it's the one that best expresses the admirable lightness firing his imagination.

There are moments of exceptional power in this series of backward glances, reminiscent—as is the author's chosen title—of the art of Ivan Turgenev, in books like *Mumu, First Love*, or the posthumously published *Prose Poems*. With Modiano, we find the same discreet, almost casual depth, the same humor, the same solitary peculiarity. The settings radiate a muted anxiety, like the apartment of Doctor Genia Karvé, with that disturbingly nostalgic line, "Happy days once more."

In cruel, precise strokes, Modiano brushes the portraits of lost women—or rather, *loose* women, in every sense of the word—who haunt the memory of the wartime generation: Martine, blinded by love, who falls prey to a con man named Baby; Arlette d'Alwyn, around whom floats a slight whiff of ruin.

This murky world, a world superficial to the point of irresponsibility, so self-absorbed that it tips into evil, is the world that has engendered every tragedy; it lets itself be carried by the tide of history without playing any part in it, like a straw on the waves. Though it may be as vain and insignificant as those old façades in rich neighborhoods, this is the world we enter into here, to discover its tortuous weft and often venomous charm.

It is a world that we cannot view with indifference, for Modiano shows it through the pitiless but generous eyes of adolescence. Valvert, the tony, somewhat vacant boarding school—targeted by the inevitable march of time; fated, as we know from the first line, not to survive the modern age—becomes the proverbial laboratory, much like Raymond Roussel's *Locus Solus*, in which the contemporary mythos was invented.

What redeems this despicable world is the presence of childhood, the childhood that remains within each of us—not a preciously preserved golden age, but the kind of childhood that knows how to observe and judge, the dark-eyed childhood that Colette writes about, which reduces adults' passions and ambitions to nil, along with their hunger for gold and their grandiose follies.

The passages of *Such Fine Boys* in which Modiano describes the tender bond between the youthful narrator and Little Jewel, who has been abandoned and abused by her overambitious mother, are among the loveliest pages written in the French language in the second half of the twentieth century.

If you haven't yet read this novel, or haven't read it in a long time, come inside without further delay, for it holds many a key to Modiano's secretive and compelling body of work.

J. M. G. Le Clézio
April 1999

Such Fine Boys

I.

A wide gravel drive rose in a gentle slope to the Castle. But what surprised you at first, to your right, in front of the infirmary, was the white flagpole with the French tricolor flapping at the top. Every morning, one of us hoisted the flag up the pole, after Mr. Jeanschmidt had given the order:

"Platoon—atten-*tion!*"

The flag rose slowly. Mr. Jeanschmidt stood at attention with us. His deep voice broke the silence.

"At ease . . . About, *left* . . . Forward, *march!*"

In quickstep, we followed the wide driveway to the Castle.

I believe Mr. Jeanschmidt wanted to acclimate us—accidental children, who belonged nowhere—to the benefits of discipline and the comfort of a homeland. Every November 11, we would join in the town ceremonies. We assembled in ranks on the Castle patio, wearing our navy blue blazers with matching knit ties. Pedro Jeanschmidt—we had nicknamed our principal Pedro—gave the departure signal. We marched in quickstep down the drive, Pedro leading the way, followed by his pupils in descending order of height. At the head of each class were the three tallest: one carried flowers, another the French flag, the third our school banner, gold triangle on midnight blue. Over

time, most of my schoolmates served as standard-bearer: Echevarietta, Charell, McFowles, Desoto, Newman, Karvé, Moncef
el Okbi, Corcuera, Archibald, Firouz, Monterey, Coemtzopou-
los, who was half-Greek and half-Ethiopian . . . We marched
through the gate and crossed the old stone bridge over the Bièvre
River. Then we came to the town hall, formerly the home of the
textile magnate Oberkampf; his oxidized bronze statue stood on
its marble pedestal and watched through hollow eyes as we filed
past. After that was the railroad crossing. When the barrier was
down and the signal announced an oncoming train, we stood
still, at attention. The barrier creaked upright and Pedro jerked
his arm forward, like a mountain guide. We resumed our march.
Along the town's main street, children on the sidewalks cheered
us as if we were soldiers home from the war. We went to join the
real veterans gathered on the church square. Once more Pedro
barked the order to stand at attention. And one after another, the
students stepped forward to lay a wreath at the base of the Monu-
ment to the Unknown Soldier.

■

The Valvert School for Boys occupied the former property of a
certain Valvert, who had been an intimate of the comte d'Artois
and accompanied him into exile under the Revolution. Later, as
an officer in the Russian army, he fell at the Battle of Austerlitz,
fighting against his own countrymen in the uniform of the Izmai-

lovsky Regiment. All that remained of him was his name and a pink marble colonnade, now half ruined, at the back of the park.

My schoolmates and I were raised under that man's morose tutelage, and perhaps some of us, without realizing it, still bear the traces.

■

Pedro's house was set back from the foot of the drive, opposite the flagpole and the infirmary. His thatched cottage with its vivid colors reminded us of Snow White and the Seven Dwarfs. An impeccable flowerbed surrounded it, tended by Pedro himself.

He invited me in only once, the evening when I'd run away. I had spent long hours wandering around the Champs-Elysées, searching for who knows what, before I gave up and went back to the school. The class monitor had said Pedro was expecting me.

The highly polished furniture, the floor tiles, china, and small tinted windowpanes, all lit by a single lamp, were like something out of a Dutch interior. Pedro sat behind a large antique wooden desk, smoking a pipe.

"Why did you run away this afternoon? Are you unhappy here?"

The question surprised me.

"No . . . Not particularly."

"I'll let it go this time. But you're grounded."

The two of us had remained facing each other in silence for

several minutes, Pedro puffing thoughtfully on his pipe. He saw me to the door.

"Let's not do it again."

He gave me a sad, affectionate look.

"If you feel like talking, come see me. I wouldn't want you to be unhappy."

I walked up the driveway toward the Castle, then looked back. Pedro was standing on his porch. Normally, everything about him—his chiseled face, stocky build, pipe, and Alpine Swiss accent—exuded strength. But that evening, for the first time, he had seemed worried. Because I had run away? Perhaps he was thinking about our future, after we'd left Valvert— his realm, increasingly surrounded by a hostile, unfathomable world—when he, Pedro, could no longer protect us.

■

The driveway cut across the wide expanse of lawn where we spent afternoon and evening recess and played field hockey. At the far end of the lawn, near the wall surrounding the property, stood a bunker tall as a brownstone, left over from the war, when the estate had housed the Luftwaffe general staff. Behind it, a dirt path that skirted the surrounding wall wended its way to Pedro's cottage and the main gate. A bit farther down from the bunker was an old greenhouse converted into a gymnasium.

Often, in my dreams, I follow the driveway up to the Castle, passing a brown shed on my right: the hut where we changed into our sports gear. Finally, I arrive at the graveled patio of the Castle, a white two-story building with a porch ringed by a handrail. It had been built at the end of the nineteenth century, modeled on the castle at Malmaison. I climb the porch steps and push open the door, which automatically clicks shut behind me. I am in the black-and-white checkerboard foyer that leads to the two dining halls.

From the left wing of the Castle, which we called the "New Wing"—Pedro had built it in the early fifties—a path sloped down to the Swiss Yard, which our principal had named after his native land. I don't take this path in my dreams, but instead enter the labyrinth, which was off-limits to us, and in which only Pedro and the faculty were allowed. A narrow, leafy passage, circular clearings and bowers, stone benches, the scent of privet. The labyrinth, too, opened onto the Swiss Yard.

This yard was surrounded, as if in a village square, by the mismatched houses used for classrooms or dormitories, with bedrooms shared by five or six of us. Each house had its own name: the Hermitage, which looked like a country manor; the Nursery, a Norman villa with half-timbering; the Green Pavilion; the Home; the Source, with its minaret; the Studio; the Gully; and the Chalet, which could have passed for one of those old Alpine hotels that some eccentric millionaire had transplanted here piece by piece. At the back of the yard, they had converted a former stable with turret into a movie house and theater.

We would assemble in the yard at around noon, before heading in ranks up to the Castle for lunch, or whenever Pedro wanted to make an important announcement. We would say, "Swiss Yard, such-and-such o'clock," and these sibylline words were meaningful only to us.

I lived in every house on that yard, but my favorite was the Green Pavilion. It owed its name to the ivy eating away at its façade. Under the balcony of the Green Pavilion, we would take shelter from the rain during recess. An outside staircase with a finely tooled wooden ramp led to the upper floors. The first floor housed the library. For a long time, I shared a room on the second floor with Charell, McFowles, Newman, and the future actor Edmond Claude.

On spring evenings, we would sit near the open window in the Green Pavilion and smoke. We had to wait until very late, when all was quiet. We had our choice of two windows: one looked out on the Swiss Yard, where Pedro sometimes made his rounds, wearing a tartan robe and puffing on his pipe; and the other, smaller one, scarcely more than a dormer, overlooked a country road that ran alongside the Bièvre.

Edmond Claude and Newman wanted to get a rope, so we could let ourselves out and down the wall. McFowles and Charell had decided we would catch the train, whose whistle we heard every night at the same hour.

But where did that train go?

II.

Some of our teachers lived in one or other of the houses on the Swiss Yard, and Pedro had appointed them "captains" of those buildings. They were responsible for keeping order with the help of "cadets," students recruited from the junior and senior years. These cadets conducted evening "inspections," checking to see that beds were properly made, closets kept neat, shoes shined. After nine o'clock curfew, the cadets made sure everyone was asleep and no one turned his lights back on.

The captain of the Green Pavilion was our gym teacher, Mr. Kovnovitsyn, whom we called "Kovo." He didn't want any cadets under him, and no one inspected our rooms. We could turn out our lamps when we pleased. The only danger was that Pedro, on his nightly patrol of the grounds, would notice the light in our window and let go with a shrill whistle blast, like an air raid warden.

Kovo, a former tennis trainer, would give his favorite pupils one of his old business cards:

KOVNOVITSYN
Licensed Tennis Instructor
8 Villa Diez-Monin
Paris 16

A tall man with slicked-back white hair and a classic profile, he wore white cotton trousers and had a Labrador retriever named Shoura that sometimes came to visit us in our rooms. Unable to sleep, Kovo spent his nights wandering about the school's great lawn. I had watched him from my window at around two or three in the morning, slowly crossing the yard, his Lab on a leash. His cotton trousers glowed in the dark. He sometimes let go of the leash and the dog must have run off, for after a while we would hear him calling:

"Shoooooooooooo-raaa . . ."

And that call, endlessly repeated until dawn, sometimes near, sometimes far, echoed like the wail of an oboe.

I don't know whether Captain Kovnovitsyn still walks his dog at night. I saw only one of our teachers again, a decade or so after leaving school: our chemistry teacher, Lafaure. I heard, Edmond, that you, too, ran into Lafaure . . .

Yes, I did. That evening, the audience had been no better or worse than in the other provincial towns where our touring company stopped. At intermission, in the minuscule dressing room I shared with Sylvestre-Bel, someone handed me a calling card:

> Dear Edmond Claude, your former
> chemistry teacher at the Valvert School,
>
> LAFAURE,
>
> requests the pleasure of your company, if
> possible, for a light supper after the show.

"An admirer?" Sylvestre-Bel asked.

I couldn't tear my eyes away from that yellowed card, in the middle of which the name LAFAURE was engraved in ash-gray letters.

"No, an old friend of the family."

And when it was my turn to go onstage, for my few minutes and five lines, I heard in the silence a murmur from the front rows: "Bravo! Bravo!" I recognized it immediately: Lafaure's sepulchral voice, which we used to make fun of in class and because of which we had nicknamed him "Death's Head."

Five soft but distinct taps on the door of our dressing room. They sounded like Morse code. I opened it. Lafaure.

"Am I disturbing you?"

He stood there with his white crew cut, stiff and shy in a navy blue suit with peg-leg trousers that stopped well above the ankles and exposed two huge black rubber-soled shoes. He used to wear shoes like that at school, and those clodhoppers of his gave him the sluggish tread of a sleepwalker.

His face had grown gaunt and wrinkled, but his skin was the same chalk white as ever.

"Do come in, Monsieur Lafaure."

In that cramped dressing room, Sylvestre-Bel was sitting on our one rickety cane chair, removing his makeup over a cardboard washbasin, while I stood pressed against Lafaure, who had closed the door behind him.

"This is my former chemistry teacher . . ."

Sylvestre-Bel turned around and gave Lafaure a supercilious nod. Out of vanity, he had not yet removed his stage toupee, which made him look even younger: at sixty, he could pass for thirty-five, like certain Americans who, with their sunbathing, diet, and skin care, are like youthful mummies.

"Sir, you were outstanding," Lafaure said to him.

He pulled the program from his jacket pocket and leafed through it. Large portraits of our star and our director in the front, followed by smaller photos of Sylvestre-Bel and the other cast members; mine was the size of a postage stamp.

"I would be most grateful if you would autograph this," Lafaure said to Sylvestre-Bel, handing him the program open to the page with his photo.

"With pleasure. And your name . . . ?"

"Lafaure. Thierry Lafaure."

And while my friend laboriously penned his inscription: "For Mr. Thierry Lafaure, with best wishes from Sylvestre-Bel," Lafaure and I hovered over his shoulder.

"Thank you."

"The least I can do," said Sylvestre-Bel, puffing out his chest.

■

So as not to keep my old teacher waiting, I didn't bother removing my makeup. We left the theater. A misty rain was falling.

"I reserved a table at the Armes de la Ville," Lafaure said. "It's the only place that stays open after ten."

We walked, he with the same stiff gait he'd had at the school and I with my head bowed, for fear my makeup would run in the drizzle. The sucking noise of his rubber soles and his pale yellow raincoat made him seem positively ghostly.

"Which hotel are you staying at?" he asked me.

"The Armoric."

"And are you leaving tomorrow?"

"Yes. On the tour bus."

"A pity you can't stay longer . . ."

His pace quickened, like a windup toy that had just been given another twist, and I feared I might lose him. The yellow coat and rhythmic squeaks of his shoes would be my only reference points in the dark. Suddenly, we came upon the glass front of a large, empty restaurant, its mirrors, woodwork, and leather shining under the globe-shaped lights.

"I reserved a table for two," Lafaure said in his graveyard voice to a man with a brown mustache behind the bar.

The man gestured grumpily toward the empty tables.

"Take your pick."

Lafaure pulled me toward a table in the back.

"We'll have peace and quiet here," he said.

Farther on, through an open swing door, came clouds of smoke, shouts, and laughter. Now and then a silhouette armed with a pool cue flitted by the doorway.

"Sometimes I play that game," Lafaure said sadly. "There isn't much to do around here."

I had a hard time imagining Lafaure playing pool. Stiff as he was, how could he bend over? I pictured his body snapping at a ninety-degree angle with a sound like a car jack and him bracing his chin on the pool table so he could keep in position long enough to take the shot.

"I think I'll go for the onion and anchovy pizza," he said. "How about you?"

"I'll have the same."

"They're excellent here."

A young man of about twenty, with blond ringlets and green eyes, had stationed himself next to our table and was waiting to take our order, arms folded, gazing sardonically at Lafaure.

"Stéphane, bring us two onion and anchovy pizzas."

"Very good, Monsieur Lafaure."

Stéphane nodded ceremoniously, his exaggerated gesture radiating insolence.

"A nice boy," said Lafaure. "He's trying to improve his mind. I'm giving him history books to read. He has an artistic streak, like you. He'd like to be a film actor . . ."

His features tensed. Apparently, this was a sensitive topic.

"Maybe he can break into the movies. Don't you think he has a face like an angel?"

So much anxiety showed through the question that I didn't dare answer. I sensed something sordid and hurtful between that boy and Lafaure.

"Anyway, Edmond, I'm very glad to see you again."

So he remembered my name.

"How long has it been? Let's see . . . Thirteen years, I think . . . Thirteen years already . . . Well, you haven't changed a bit . . ."

"Neither have you, Monsieur Lafaure."

"Oh, please . . . !"

He let out a sigh and rubbed his brush-cut hair. Under the harsh neon lights, his face was even gaunter and more creased than in the dressing room, and his skin dotted with age spots.

"Ever since I retired and left the Valvert School, I've been living here with my older sister. I would gladly have invited you to the house, but my sister is an early bird and she gets very cranky . . ."

"Do you still keep in touch with Valvert?"

"There is no more Valvert. The property was sold to a real estate developer who tore down all the buildings. It's sad, don't you think?"

I took in the news with detachment, but the next day it left me feeling empty, like the silence and dust above a demolished wall.

"Mr. Kovnovitsyn writes me now and again. He lives in Sainte-Geneviève-des-Bois. Do you remember him?"

"Of course. A really good guy . . . Kovo . . ."

"Right, Kovo. And I know you used to call me 'Death's Head.'"

He smiled, apparently with no hard feelings—a wide, skeletal grin that justified our nickname for him.

The young man with green eyes brought our pizzas.

"They're not overcooked, are they, Stéphane?"

"No, no, certainly not, Monsieur Lafaure."

"Stéphane, this is a friend of mine from Paris. He's an actor. He was in a play tonight in town . . . I'm asking if he has any pointers for you."

"Thank you, Monsieur Lafaure."

He gave Lafaure such an insolent stare that I felt bad for the man.

"And now, Stéphane, let us get back to our conversation . . ."

Perhaps my former teacher wanted to make the boy jealous, or earn his respect, by being seen with an "actor."

"I often think about Valvert," said Lafaure.

"Me too."

We tried to slice into our pizzas, which were dry as rock gardens.

"These were baked way too long, but I don't like to say anything. I'm . . . I'm a little afraid of him."

He looked over at the other end of the room, where the young man was standing.

"I'll tell him we met in Paris . . . Whatever you do, don't bring up Valvert . . ."

The Valvert School. It seemed very far away in this deserted restaurant, sitting with our fossilized pizzas, in this dull provincial town where we didn't even have a place to remove our makeup. An abandoned realm that one visits in a dream: The great lawn and the bunker in the moonlight. The leafy maze. The tennis courts. The woods. The rhododendrons. Oberkampf's tomb . . .

"And have you heard from any of the other students?" I asked him.

"Six years ago I had a postcard from Jim Echevarietta. You remember him, right? A dark-haired boy. He went back home to Argentina . . ."

Apparently that fact made Lafaure deeply sad.

"Argentina is such a long way from here . . ."

Echevarietta. We used to sit next to each other in class. During math, he would furtively raise the lid of his desk and show me photos of his polo ponies, one by one.

"What about you, Edmond? Have you seen any of your old classmates?"

"Yes, McFowles . . . Daniel Desoto . . ."

"I don't remember this Desoto."

"Desoto was kind of like Echevarietta. His father used to give him a thousand francs a week in pocket money . . ."

"Yes . . . There were some strange fellows at that school. All of them damaged by their family situations. Don't you think, Edmond?"

We gave up on eating our pizzas, which tasted like warm chewing gum.

"How did you hear I was in a play?"

"I get all the tour programs and I saw your name."

My sorry little name, in tiny letters at the bottom of the poster, half the size of Sylvestre-Bel's.

Lafaure squeezed my arm and, as with his laugh and voice, his grip was like a skeleton's.

"I always thought you'd do something artistic . . . Already, back at school . . ."

The shouts of the pool players next door drowned out his voice. I cast a furtive glance in the mirror behind him. Despite my worries, I didn't look like a clown, even if the foundation gave me a fake-looking tan, like someone who spent his days on a yacht, and my eyebrows were too black and too arched. But it wasn't excessive, though I followed Sylvestre-Bel's advice and put on my makeup the old-fashioned way, using Leichner grease sticks with their gaudy colors, and plenty of cocoa butter to take it off.

"Monsieur Lafaure, I apologize for the makeup but I didn't want to keep you waiting . . ."

After all, he looked made-up too. His skin was white as a mime's.

"Nonsense, Edmond, it suits you."

He looked me over with such admiration. I would never have a better audience than that old chemistry teacher, for whom, already, back at school . . . Alas, with advancing age comes the realization that one won't play major roles, but rather walk-ons, cameos. There is nothing dishonorable about being one of the profession's obscure nobodies. Sylvestre-Bel often said so, he who had spent forty years specializing in minor parts: valet or maître d'. He flitted by, terse, elegant, erect, imperious like the sound of his name. His fleeting appearances were the secret of his eternal youth, or so he claimed.

"Do you know, Edmond, I still have that transistor radio . . ."

Lafaure had leaned toward me and whispered those words.

It took me a few seconds to understand, then a memory came flooding back, with summery hues and the scent of underbrush.

It was the end of the academic term. We had teased our chemistry teacher mercilessly all year long and now felt bad about it. So we decided to pool our resources and buy him a parting gift, and our buddy McFowles had been deputized to bring back from the United States, where he often went with his grandmother, the best transistor radio he could find. We had presented it to Lafaure at the beginning of chemistry class. He was so moved that he suggested we skip class and go for a long stroll around the school grounds.

We walked in a group, Lafaure at the center, and McFowles showed him how to tune in the various French and foreign frequencies. At fifteen, McFowles was already nearly six-foot-three. He went in for hazardous sports, which would later cost him his life. But that day, with his gangly movements, he showed Lafaure how to use the radio.

We walked in the sun across the great lawn and followed a path bordered by clumps of rhododendrons. The fitness trail. The tennis courts. And we entered the woods . . .

The next day was the start of summer break. I can still hear the snatches of music from the radio, our voices, Lafaure's marking time like the sighs of a bass, McFowles's booming laughter . . .

"By the way, Edmond, before I forget, I wanted to get your autograph as well."

Abruptly, Lafaure thrust the red-and-gold playbill at me. He furrowed his brow, and I could see there were tears in his eyes—strange, for that skeletal face.

My photo was next to Sylvestre-Bel's, but so, so small . . . You could hardly make out my features. I wrote, "For Mr. Lafaure, in remembrance of Valvert, from his ex-student Edmond Claude."

We got up from the table and crossed the dining room. Lafaure walked ahead of me with his mechanical stride, his coat carefully folded over his stiff arm. The young man who had served our pizzas was leaning gracefully against the bar. He fixed Lafaure with the same stare as before, as if confident of his power over the man. Lafaure bowed his head.

The rain was falling much harder now. I helped him on with his yellow raincoat. The lights inside the restaurant went off. We had no umbrella, and so Lafaure and I stood there, side by side, in silence, beneath the metal awning of the Armes de la Ville.

■

Well, Edmond, it so happens that one Christmas Eve, I was with my two small daughters at the entrance to the Rex cinema, waiting to see a Disney movie. The line was made up entirely of parents and children. Several feet ahead of us, a very stiff man with white hair caught my attention. He was alone, wrapped in a yellow raincoat and dust-gray scarf. He cast furtive glances at the children around him, as if searching for one in particular with whom he might start a conversation. Our eyes met. It was Lafaure.

He jerked his face away, like someone caught red-handed. I saw him discreetly leave the line. Was he afraid that too sudden a movement might draw attention and that someone might collar him? Had he recognized me? I would have liked to ask him—you know I would have, Edmond—but Thierry Lafaure was already fading like a ghost into the crowds on the boulevard.

III.

Every Thursday, Gino Bordin, our guitar instructor, arrived on the bus that left from Porte de Saint-Cloud. I've since learned that he lived in Montmartre at the time, at 8 Rue Audran, but that information doesn't do me much good, as he's no longer in the phone book.

Bordin always wore a midnight blue suit, embellished by a pocket square and a pale silk tie. He wore glasses with thin silver frames, and his hair, also silver, was slicked back, like Kovo's. At around noon on Thursdays, he would walk quickly up the driveway to the Castle, brown guitar case in his left hand. He ate in the cafeteria, at a table in back. Sadly, I never managed to sit at his table, but all through the meal I watched him. He often had his tablemates in stitches. I knew all his stories by heart. He'd introduced Hawaiian-style guitar to France, which was his claim to fame.

Bordin had no classroom at his disposal. They didn't even let him use the music room, on the ground floor of the New Wing. They had relegated him to a wooden bench in the foyer, in front of the monumental staircase that led to the Castle's upper floors. There, in the drafts from outside and the dim light, he gave his half-tolerated lessons.

It was surely the limited number of Bordin's students that kept him in such low esteem. For a long time, there were only two, Michel Karvé and me. But every Thursday afternoon at the end of class, at my urging and Karvé's, a small group of acolytes would gather round to hear Bordin play: Edmond Claude, Charell, Portier, Desoto, McFowles, El Okbi, Newman . . . The other students were let outside on those afternoons, and they scattered over the lawn and playing fields. But we preferred to hang out with Bordin.

When it approached six o'clock, he would play a slow, poignant tune, "How High the Moon." That meant it was time to leave. Karvé and I walked him to the bus stop: Pedro had given us special permission to exit through the gate with our teacher and linger awhile in the open air. The three of us waited on the sidewalk in front of the public park. Bordin absently stroked the neck of his guitar, which he leaned against his leg. He gave us each a friendly hug.

"A gioved', amici miei . . ."

He climbed into the bus and always sat in back, resting his guitar on the seat beside him. As the bus passed over the railroad crossing, he waved to us.

When I think of the chords from Bordin's Hawaiian guitar, I imagine a breeze blowing down a sunny, empty street toward the sea. I also recall my classmate Michel Karvé. We were friendly enough, Karvé and I, but there was something about him I couldn't figure out. I'm thinking of the day when they gave us all a questionnaire: we were supposed to write down our birthdate and our parents' professions.

Karvé seemed to hesitate a moment. He gazed pensively through the window. Outside, the winter sun bathed the Swiss Yard in a soft, hazy light. He opened his desk and looked something up in the dictionary. He closed the lid. Then he took the plunge. Under the heading "Parents' Occupation," he wrote, in a beautiful, meticulous hand: "Influence peddling."

■

I checked my own dictionary to find the meaning of those words and I would have liked Michel Karvé to tell me more, but I didn't want to be nosy.

I had met his parents several times, on our days off, at his home on Avenue Victor-Hugo. They struck me as very distinguished. Doctor Genia Karvé was a tall, thin man, whose light-colored eyes made him look youthful. His wife had strawberry blond hair, the face of a lioness, eyes as light as her husband's, and the nonchalant, athletic demeanor of certain American women.

At first glance, the words "influence peddling," which remained etched in my memory in Michel Karvé's clear, precise handwriting, seemed to have little to do with this couple.

I had a better opportunity to observe them during a walk we took in the Bois de Boulogne. It was a Saturday afternoon in autumn. The gray sky, the smell of wet grass and earth . . . They were walking in front of us, side by side, and the elegant silhouettes of Dr. Karvé and his wife became associated for me with phrases like *hunting party, pheasantry, pack of hounds.*

We crossed through the Parc de Bagatelle, then reached the polo grounds via the road down below. It was growing dark. Something had struck me about Michel's parents: they never addressed a word to their son, and seemed to be completely indifferent to his presence. I also noted the contrast between my friend's clothes and those of Dr. and Mme Karvé. He wore patched corduroy trousers and an old blazer that was too large for him. No overcoat. Rubber sandals. At school, I had given him two pairs of socks, as all of his had holes in them.

Later, Michel and I were in the back seat of Dr. Karvé's big black sedan—he took no care of the vehicle and its body was spattered with mud. Dr. Karvé was smoking behind the wheel. Now and then, he and his wife exchanged a brief word. It was about people that my friend surely knew.

"We're going out this evening, Michel," Mme Karvé said. "I've left you a slice of ham in the fridge."

"Yes, Mother."

"Will that do?"

"Yes, Mother."

She'd said it in a clipped, distracted voice, and didn't turn around to face him.

■

Influence peddling. I've kept a sheet of blue letterhead with the name of Doctor Genia Karvé, "Ear, Nose, and Throat Specialist, 12 Avenue Victor-Hugo, Paris 16th, PASsy 38-80," on which the latter, in a firm hand, had prescribed some medicine for me. He examined me one evening when Michel had told him I wasn't feeling well. In his office, he had demonstrated the same courteous indifference that he usually showed his son and me. On the shelves of his library, I noticed signed photos of women, most of them in leather frames, and I inched closer for a better look.

"Those are patients as well as friends," Dr. Karvé said with a shrug, cigarette dangling from the corner of his lips.

■

Influence peddling. The day after Michel had so strangely answered the questionnaire, we saw through our classroom window Dr. Karvé's black sedan cross the Swiss Yard and turn left onto the driveway leading to the Castle. It was the first time Dr. Karvé had visited our school. Never had Michel's parents come to pick him up on our days off. Like me, Michel took the bus to Porte de Saint-Cloud. Then the metro.

My classmate hadn't blinked. He even pretended not to notice his father's car. A few moments later, one of the school monitors entered the classroom, interrupting our English lesson.

"Karvé, the principal wants to see you. He's with your father."

Michel stood up. In his old blue smock and sandals, he followed the monitor with stiff steps, like someone being led to the firing squad.

■

They had evidently shown Michel's questionnaire to Dr. Genia Karvé. What had father and son said to each other in our principal's office? It was later, much later, that I looked into it. I had been out of touch with Michel for quite some time and had no idea what might have become of him or his parents. There was no longer a Dr. Genia Karvé on Avenue Victor-Hugo.

Influence peddling. I questioned various people and searched through old newspapers, whose smell reminded me of that autumn Saturday when Michel and I had gone walking in the Bois de Boulogne, with his mother and father. On the way back, Dr. Karvé had stopped the car in Neuilly, at the corner of Avenue de Madrid.

"Well, we'll let you off here. We have to meet some friends nearby."

Michel had opened the door without a word.

"Don't forget . . . the slice of ham in the fridge . . ." Mme Karvé had said in a wan voice.

For a moment, we had stood there, staring after the car as it sped away toward the Saint-James neighborhood.

"I don't have any metro tickets," said Michel. "How about you?"

"Me neither."

"If you like, you can share my slice of ham."

He had burst out laughing. That part of the avenue was dark, and we stumbled over a pile of dead leaves in the middle of the sidewalk. The closer we got to Avenue de Neuilly, the better we could see. Lights in the windows and blazing restaurant façades. Now the dead leaves coated the sidewalk in a matted layer, sticking to people's heels. Their bitter odor was the same as that of old newspapers when you gingerly turn the brittle pages, one by one, going back in time, trying to find a picture, a name, someone's buried traces.

■

A brief article, a single column at the bottom of the page. The Karvés had appeared in court. Perhaps Michel knew. The trial had taken place two years after his birth. They had discovered, at the Karvés', furniture, paintings, and jewelry of dubious provenance. The "couple" had been sentenced to prison time, suspended, and twenty thousand francs in fines for "receiving stolen goods." The report specified that on that occasion, Mme Karvé was wearing a form-fitting turquoise dress and a white leather belt, but never once, I had to admit, did they use with regard to the doctor and his wife the term "influence peddling."

■

Were these the same people that I had met, whose graceful silhouettes glided through my memory?

I ended up in a bar on Avenue Montaigne, once frequented by the worldly, horsey set, where a former regular might have been able to enlighten me: for fifty years, he had rubbed shoulders with "everybody."

I uttered the name Mme Karvé, and a tender look flashed in his eyes, as if the name brought back his youth, or that of my classmate's mother:

"You mean Andrée the Slut?" he asked under his breath.

■

Michel and I were sitting opposite each other in the café on Avenue Victor-Hugo, facing the building where his parents lived. Since the start of the Easter holidays, he had not set foot at home. One of our classmates, Charell, had taken him in.

He was still wearing his old blazer that was too big for him, his patched corduroys, and a shirt that was missing several buttons.

"Okay, now you can go," he said.

"You're sure you won't change your mind?"

"No. Go on, I'll wait for you here."

I stood up and walked out of the café. I crossed the street, and as I passed the threshold of number 12, I felt my heart pounding. I had forgotten which floor it was and checked the list of tenants, posted on the mahogany door of the concierge's lodge.

Doctor Genia Karvé. Second floor, right.

Instead of taking the elevator I decided to climb the stairs, stopping for a long pause at each landing. At the Karvés' floor, I stood still for several minutes, leaning against the banister like a boxer against the ropes, just before the start of the match. Finally, I rang the bell.

Mme Karvé opened the door. She was wearing a hounds'-tooth tailored suit and a black blouse that nicely complemented her blond hair. She didn't seem surprised to see me.

"I've come to collect Michel's things," I said.

"Ah, I see . . . Do come in . . ."

He must have telephoned to let her know I was coming. Or was she simply so indifferent to her son's fate? We crossed the foyer. A golf bag was lying on the floor.

She opened a door at the beginning of the hallway.

"Here it is . . . His things must be in the closet . . . Excuse me for a moment."

She gave me a winning smile and vanished. I heard Dr. Karvé's voice, fairly close by. He spoke for a long time but no one answered. No doubt he was on the phone.

Michel's bedroom was so small that you had to wonder whether it was originally a storage closet. The window was disproportionately large. I rested my forehead against the pane, which let through only a crepuscular light. Yet it was two in the afternoon, and outside the sun was shining. The window overlooked a rear court narrow as a pit.

Why, in that vast apartment, which Michel had once shown me when his parents were out, had they given him this tiny room? Michel claimed he'd chosen it himself.

No sheets on the cot, only a simple plaid blanket. Michel had asked me to bring it. I opened the closet and in the navy blue sports bag from the boarding school I arranged his clothes. A few old pairs of socks, a bathing suit, a handkerchief, two sweaters, three shirts. The shirts were patched, like his corduroy trousers, and strangely enough they had a famous dress designer's label on the inside collar. They turned out to be his mother's old blouses. Michel's parents dressed him in their castoffs, and his blazer, too big for him and frayed at the edges, had belonged to his father and also came from a well-known haberdasher on Rue Marbeuf.

I could still hear Dr. Karvé's droning voice on the telephone. Now and then he burst out laughing. The door, left ajar, swung open and Mme Karvé appeared in the frame.

"So . . . How are you making out?"

She enveloped me with her smile. The light bulb in the ceiling cast her face in a harsh light, bringing out the freckles in her skin. Today I have a better sense of why that woman moved me so: a mix of frivolity and languidness that in my mind I associate with France in the eighteenth century, with satins, crystal, and the color they call "Fragonard blond."

"Did you find all of Michel's clothes?"

"Yes."

She gazed at the sports bag.

"I should have given you a suitcase . . . Do you really think Michel never wants to set foot in this house again?"

"I couldn't say."

"Anyway, let him know that he'll always be welcome here."

I picked up the sports bag and slung it over my shoulder.

"Here, take this . . . It's for Michel. A little pocket money . . ."

She handed me a rumpled hundred-franc bill.

"He's always been like that," Mme Karvé said in a distant voice, as if convinced that no one would listen and she was talking to herself. "When he was little I'd take him to the Pré Catalan and he always ran away and hid . . . Sometimes it would take me an hour to find him. Poor little Michel . . ."

She walked ahead of me into the hallway. Dr. Karvé was still on the phone, making emphatic statements in a foreign tongue.

I was already on the landing. She hesitated a moment before closing the door.

"Good-bye . . ."

She held out her arm.

I should have kissed her hand, but instead I shook it.

"Good-bye. Genia is busy in his office, but be sure to tell Michel that his father sends him a big hug . . . And so do I . . ."

I went down the stairs, eager to be back in the open air and sunlight.

Michel was waiting for me at the café, arms folded. I handed him the plaid blanket and sports bag, whose contents he rapidly verified.

"You forgot 'Happy Days Once More,'" he said.

This was a drawing cut out from an old magazine that he and I had discovered in the back of the storage closet in the Green Pavilion. The magazine dated from the same month and year we were both born, July 1945, and the drawing was an ad for Antonat port wine. A blonde woman in profile, wearing a kerchief, is sitting in a small boat. On the horizon are a lake, mountains, a white sail. And above it all, in tall, narrow type:

HAPPY DAYS ONCE MORE

The nostalgia and sundrenched mildness of those words and the drawing intrigued us both. Bordin, whose opinion we had solicited, had plucked a few languorous chords from his guitar. Michel wanted to write an entire novel, inspired by the woman with the kerchief, the lake, the mountains. It would be called *Happy Days Once More*.

"I left it in my bedside drawer," he said, disappointed. "But never mind . . ."

"Would you like me to go back up and get it?"

"No, no . . . It's not worth it. I have it here, in my head . . . The main thing is that I write that novel someday."

He laid the hundred-franc bill flat on the table.

"Your mother said that if you wanted to come back . . ."

He pretended not to hear. Outside, on the opposite sidewalk, Dr. Karvé was walking among the dapples of sunlight, dragging a golf bag. Mme Karvé emerged from the building moments later. She was wearing dark glasses that contrasted with her blond skin tone. The doctor opened the rear door of his car and wearily tossed the golf bag onto the back seat. He sat behind the wheel. Mme Karvé, still nonchalant, slid in next to him. The car started up gently.

"They're going to Mortefontaine," Michel told me.

And his voice harbored no blame, only a kind of regret.

As we rode in the metro, I tried one last time to dissuade him. He had falsified his birth certificate with whiteout to make himself three years older. Yes, his mind was made up. After that, we took the train to Athis-Mons, where the recruiting station was located.

IV.

Of all our teachers, the one we surely pleased the most was Kovo. Sport was the preferred discipline of our principal, Mr. Jeanschmidt, and we devoted three afternoons a week to it.

Often, Pedro would sit in on Kovnovitsyn's classes. He and Kovo were great friends. They had similar interests. Word was that when the school was founded, by Pedro's two older brothers, Pedro had served as gym teacher.

Field hockey was the school's traditional sport. Pedro himself chose the teams and supervised their training. But we also had an in-ground swimming pool at the edge of the great lawn. And deeper into the park, we came to the running track, the pole-vaulting area, the volleyball court, the two tennis courts, and finally the fitness trail. Kovo and Mr. Jeanschmidt called it the "Hébert trail," after a certain Hébert, the architect of a physical education method to which they both subscribed.

The plans for that "Hébert trail" had been drawn up by Jeanschmidt and Kovo a good ten years earlier. A military-style training course, filled with various obstacles: walls to scale, ropes to climb, leg lifts, barriers and hoops that we had to cross crawling forward on our elbows, pommel horses for vaulting and acrobatics . . . Very early in the morning, in the spring, we would do what

Kovo called an "Hébert course," before proceeding at a run to the flag-raising ceremony.

Those daily outdoor activities bore fruit. Our field hockey team had reached the Junior Nationals and our pole vaulters could challenge the French national team. Kovo got Jean-schmidt to agree to extra hours of gym, at the expense of other classes. And I think Pedro was right to grant him this privilege. For most of us, sports were a refuge, a way of momentarily leaving behind the difficulties of living, especially for our classmate Robert McFowles.

Kovo admired McFowles. At fifteen, he was captain of the hockey team and was equally gifted at skiing, swimming, and tennis. Bob and I had shared a room one year in the Green Pavilion and become fast friends.

He ended up getting himself killed, at around thirty, in a bobsled championship in Switzerland, but I'd had a chance to see him before then. I even happened to join him on his honeymoon. He had just gotten married to a local girl from Versailles and, not knowing where to go for their wedding trip, he had chosen a hotel near the Trianons for the month of August.

It was very hot that summer, and McFowles and his wife sunbathed on the hotel's main lawn. Anne-Marie—the brand-new Mme McFowles—wore a bright red bathing suit, while McFowles's was imitation leopard skin, which reminded me of Valvert. We liked those Tarzan swimsuits, and most of us wore them beside the school's swimming pool, a strange pool filled with black, stagnant water that we dyed with methylene blue to make it look Mediterranean. And we jury-rigged the ramshackle diving board as best we could.

Bob McFowles had met his future wife a few months earlier at a ski resort. She was working as a hotel receptionist. Love at first sight. Their wedding had been celebrated in Versailles, where Anne-Marie's father owned a shop on Rue Carnot.

A girl of average height, with blond hair and big blue eyes. Her timid grace reminded me of certain eighteenth-century portraits, like the one of Louise de Polastron. Anne-Marie was every inch a Frenchwoman, and it made for a harmonious contrast with Bob McFowles's slightly unpolished demeanor, his height and heavy, lanky gait.

Bob's only family was an American grandmother, one Mrs. Strauss, the creator of the Harriet Strauss line of cosmetics. Back in the Valvert days, he would spend his Christmas and Easter holidays with her on the Riviera, and for the long summer vacation she would take him to America. For the rest of the year, Bob never left school, not even on our days out. Every week he received a letter from his grandmother, his name typed in red on the fawn-colored envelope.

In those days, Harriet Strauss beauty products were displayed in the windows of perfume shops, and I admired them while thinking of my old schoolmate. Those products have since disappeared, but in the summer of the McFowleses' honeymoon, Harriet Strauss lipstick and foundations still sat beside their rivals from Max Factor and Elizabeth Arden on the makeup counter. They ensured a comfortable living for Bob, to whom, on his twenty-first birthday, his grandmother had transferred all of her shares in Harriet Strauss.

We were lying on the lawn in our bathing suits, Bob, Anne-Marie, and I, and McFowles was sipping orangeade through a straw.

"Too bad," he said. "The only thing missing in this place is the sea . . ."

And in fact, under the strong sun, the white façade, the tables with their red umbrellas, the French doors running along the gallery, and the orange canvas awnings made the hotel look like a seaside resort.

"Don't you think, old man, that the only thing missing is the sea?"

At the time I didn't pay much attention to McFowles's remark, or to his dreamy expression, but it was from that afternoon that the "malaise"—I can't think of another word for it—began to weigh on us.

And yet, McFowles was in a charming mood over lunch on the hotel terrace. He had invited Mr. Lebon, his father-in-law, a man with white hair and a mustache, also very French, whose delicate face could have been painted by Clouet. McFowles clearly intimidated him, and Lebon articulated his syllables when speaking to his son-in-law, as if talking to a foreigner. But Bob's extreme kindness slowly put him at ease. My classmate asked about his business and listened attentively. This was the Robert McFowles I'd known at Valvert, moody but able to engage with others and win their affections with his warm gaze and his thoughtfulness. Anne-Marie seemed delighted by how well her father and Bob were getting along.

Coffee was served. McFowles made a wide sweep of his arm that took in the terrace, deserted except for us, and the hotel lawn.

"I think there's only one thing missing here," he said to Anne-Marie's father. "Guess what it is, Dad."

Lebon gave an abashed smile.

"I . . . I'm not sure . . ."

Anne-Marie no doubt recalled Bob's declaration from the day before. She burst out laughing. That laugh, when I recall the subsequent turn of events, makes my blood run cold.

"Yes . . . There's something missing here," McFowles said in a serious voice.

"Guess, Daddy," Anne-Marie insisted.

Lebon knit his brow.

"No . . . Honestly . . . I can't see anything."

"It's missing the sea," said McFowles, in a grave tone that surprised the three of us.

"Oh, indeed," said Lebon. "It's the perfect weather for the seashore."

"But sadly, there is no seashore in Versailles," said McFowles.

He suddenly seemed devastated. Lebon shot me a puzzled glance.

"Bob really likes the sea," I stammered.

Anne-Marie looked mortified.

"Anyway, we're planning on going to the seashore at the end of the month," she said.

But Bob had raised his head and his face was lit with a child-like smile.

"You can't ask the impossible, right, Dad?"

A few days later, an old, green American convertible pulled to a halt at the edge of the lawn, in a loud crunch of gravel. It was McFowles's car, which two friends had brought over from Paris. He introduced them to me: James Mourenz, a boy our age with a blond brush-cut and Swiss nationality, McFowles's team-mate for the bobsled championships that he competed in every winter; and Edouard Agam, a short, dark-haired man of about fifty. I could never tell whether he was Lebanese, Egyptian, or a Syrian living in Egypt, which would have accounted for his flawless French and Christian first name. Agam had led a dance band on the Riviera. McFowles had met him in Geneva, when his career was on the wane.

Those two men were Bob's parasites, but ingenuous Anne-Marie hadn't the slightest suspicion. They never left my friend's side, like two bodyguards or court jesters. James Mourenz's laugh, his scars, his habit of clapping you on the shoulder, of get-ting defensive and hopping around you like a boxer, amused me at first. And I was susceptible to Edouard Agam's courtesies. Bob had confided that they were his two best friends—his "pals," as the American expression put it.

And things might have gone differently, the days might have followed each other without a care, if it hadn't been for the sea. McFowles talked about it constantly. "Didn't you see the sea? I'm sure it's high tide. What color is the sea today? Can't you smell the sea?" Mourenz and Agam, aiming to please, had immediately joined in. Agam sang us Charles Trenet's "Beyond the Sea," strumming a guitar. Mourenz claimed that the sea reached to the edge of the hotel terrace and wanted us to admire his dives. He, too, wore a leopard-skin swimsuit and, standing on the balustrade, he took deep breaths that swelled his chest. Then he dove headfirst onto the lawn, jerking himself upright at the last instant.

"Too cold?" asked McFowles.

"No, this morning it's fine," Mourenz answered, shaking his arms and slicking back his hair as if he'd just plunged in. "The water's perfect."

A casual observer might have taken this for a simple gag, but nonetheless felt some concern the day when Mourenz, deeming that the terrace balustrade made too low a diving board, decided to plunge from the hotel's main portico. This plan won McFowles's and Edouard Agam's enthusiastic endorsement; Anne-Marie and I didn't dare object.

"Go ahead, jump right in," said McFowles. "The water's deep at that spot . . ."

With a stepladder, Mourenz hiked himself onto the upper terrace, which was more than nine feet above ground. Agam, poker-faced, hummed "Beyond the Sea." The hotel porter and one of the bellboys followed the scene, spellbound.

"I will now perform for you the swan dive," said Mourenz.

He grimaced defiantly. McFowles had told me that his daring, at the bobsled competitions in Saint-Moritz, had earned him the nickname Suicide James.

"Go on," said McFowles. "The waves have died down. It's like a swimming pool. Show us your swan dive."

Mourenz, standing stiffly on the portico railing, lips pressed tight, took a deep breath. With a sudden lunge, he launched himself up high, arms outstretched. You would have sworn he was going to break his neck, but in a fraction of a second he clutched his knees to his chest and fell onto the soft grass in the "egg position" that the skier Jean Vuarnet had illustrated so effectively in the early sixties. We applauded. Only McFowles remained stone-faced.

"Next time, you'll dive from higher up and when there are waves," he said coldly.

From then on, every morning, Suicide James dove. Jack-knife, from a table he had set up on the hotel terrace; gainer flips; reverse dives. And each time, these demonstrations concluded with the usual quips — "the water's fine," "you should come in, too" — until the day when he slightly fractured his forearm. He wore the arm in a sling, a white silk scarf that McFowles had given him, and from morning till night his entire outfit was that scarf and his leopard-skin swimsuit.

"You won't be able to swim anymore, poor fellow," said Mc-Fowles. "It's really a shame, in this heat . . ."

But even with his arm in a cast, Mourenz had not lost his enthusiasm. He wanted to send away to Paris for an outboard and water skis that they could use in the Grand Canal of Versailles. McFowles had an orange-colored beach tent, and he obtained the hotel manager's permission to set it up on the lawn. The five of us stood around the tent.

"It smells like the sea," said Mourenz.

"Shall we take advantage of low tide to go for a walk?" asked McFowles.

He leaned toward Anne-Marie.

"I'm going to gather you some lovely shells, darling . . ."

She gave him a worried look. I could tell the joke was beginning to frighten her. No doubt she would have preferred to spend some time alone with Bob on their honeymoon.

A kind of bitterness and lassitude overcame McFowles. The good-natured banter had given way to ill-tempered remarks, like, "You think we're going to have to wait much longer for that fucking sea?"

He turned to Mourenz.

"So, you're not diving today? You chickening out?"

I suggested we visit our old Valvert School, right near Versailles.

"Fine, as long as there's some ocean."

One evening I'd managed to get them to take a walk along

the Grand Canal, and we had arrived at the far end, where the meadows begin. Cows were grazing. The horizon was unobstructed, and it was as if those meadows overlooked the sea. I couldn't help saying so to Bob.

"You're right," he stated, "but it's a mirage. The farther you go, the more the water recedes."

Agam, behind us, was playing the accordion. Mourenz now had only a cast on his wrist. Anne-Marie was anxious.

That night, at around three in the morning, I was awoken by the telephone. Anne-Marie. She said that Bob was prostrate in the hotel lobby and wouldn't come up to bed. From the sound of her voice, I could tell she was crying.

We both went downstairs to find him. He was sitting on one of the couches in the grand hall. We sat beside him.

"You'll have to forgive me . . . I'm still waiting for that goddamn sea. It's really no fun, you know . . ."

He burst out laughing, but there was something forced about that laugh. Anne-Marie flashed me a desperate look. No, he wasn't drunk, as she thought. He didn't need alcohol to put himself in that state.

I could see that with all her love for McFowles and all her kindness, she was searching for an explanation. What could I tell her? That Bob wasn't a bad man—far from it—but a sensitive, guileless boy who was looking for stability, otherwise he wouldn't have chosen a girl like her? Unfortunately, we, the veterans of Valvert, were prone to inexplicable bouts of melancholy, waves of sadness that we tried to ward off each in our own way. As our chemistry teacher Mr. Lafaure used to say, we all had a "touch" of it.

The sun rose. I watched the dappled light on the walls of the grand hall, gently caressed by the shadows of the foliage. A fly had come to rest on Anne-Marie's white trousers, just above the knee.

V.

Every other Saturday at 9 p.m. we would assemble in the Swiss Yard before filing into the small movie theater, where we could choose our places from among the dark wooden folding seats in the orchestra and balcony.

Pedro needed two new projectionists to step in on short notice for the former team of Yotlande and Bourdon, who were in eleventh grade. My friend Daniel Desoto and I had volunteered, and for several afternoons our two older classmates had taught us how to use the equipment. Then Yotlande was expelled and Bourdon also left school, so Desoto and I found ourselves permanently assigned to our new jobs.

The students would sit in the small auditorium with its ochre walls, which looked just like some neighborhood cinema. The screen, attached to a removable panel, concealed the stage where, once a semester, a theater troupe performed a show, and where at the end of the year Pedro gave out the scholastic achievement awards.

After a moment, Mr. Jeanschmidt made his entrance, followed by Kovnovitsyn and his Labrador on a leash. Two seats were permanently reserved for them, fifth row orchestra, near the aisle. Pedro and Kovo's entrance was greeted in silence, sometimes broken by discreet applause. Kovo's dog lay down in the middle of the aisle, in a stiff sphinxlike position, head slightly raised toward the screen.

Desoto and I, in the projection booth, waited for Pedro's signal. He raised his left arm and brought it down sharply, as if swatting away a fly. The show could begin.

A documentary or cartoon, to start. I turned the lights back on. The folding seats clacked shut. The students went out for a moment to the Swiss Yard, but Pedro, Kovo, and the dog remained in their places. A few friends joined us in the projection booth. I rang the bell to announce the end of intermission. And once more, Pedro's imperious gesture.

We watched *The Man in the White Suit, Passport to Pimlico*, and other films whose titles I've forgotten, but the one that appeared on the program most often—at least once a semester—was *Archer's Crossing*.

A manor, a blonde countess, her little daughter, the gamekeeper's lodge, a painter in love with the countess, the sound of a harmonium in the night, a wolf baying at the moon . . .

Kovnovitsyn's Labrador, its ears pricked up, answered with a plaintive bark.

The child who played the part of the countess's daughter was called Little Jewel, or at least that was her name in the credits. The first time *Archer's Crossing* was shown in our movie theater, Pedro and Kovnovitsyn were with a man of about forty, to whom Pedro occasionally gave an affectionate pat on the shoulder. When the show was over, our principal asked everyone to remain seated. He stood and gestured toward the man next to him.

"I'd like to introduce you to a former student of this school. He has come specially this evening because he knew one of the actresses in the film."

From then on, every time we showed *Archer's Crossing* at Valvert, the man attended the projection. On those Saturdays, his car was parked in front of the Castle and he ate in the dining hall at Pedro's table.

He was a man of average height, with light brown hair and lively eyes. He worked in import-export. As luck would have it, I too sat at Pedro's table that year. The two of them spoke about the past and various "alums."

"Do you find Valvert very different?" Pedro asked.

"No. Valvert is still Valvert."

Several students had been lost during the war, among them a certain Johnny, of whom Pedro kept a fond memory.

"Come back next month," he said. "We'll show *Archer's Crossing* again."

I believe Pedro showed the film as often as he did to make his "alum" happy. The man had said, "It's awfully kind of you to let me see Little Jewel again, Monsieur Jeanschmidt . . ."

At the end of the meal, the alum offered us cigarettes. It was against the rules, but our principal, for once, turned a blind eye. And one evening when we asked him about Little Jewel, he agreed to satisfy our curiosity, and Pedro's.

■

Yes, I can say that my life, to this day, has been just a long, fruitless search for Little Jewel. I met her after I left Valvert, when I was taking acting lessons. Of all the students in the Marivaux Course, not one made a career in show business, except for this overweight fellow we used to call Pudgy.

All my memories of Marivaux are set against a backdrop of winter and nighttime. I was eighteen, and three times a week I attended what our teacher called "group sessions." She was a former member of the Comédie Française, and she'd set up the Marivaux Course in a storefront near Place de l'Etoile: "Your entree to theater and film, music hall and cabaret," the brochure said.

Against that backdrop of winter and nighttime, I can still picture those group sessions, from eight to ten-thirty in the evening. After class, we'd chat awhile, me, Pudgy, and the others, before dispersing into the blackout. One evening, on the street corner, I ran into Johnny, an old classmate from Valvert. He was looking for work in the film studios. I suggested he take the class with us, but I never heard from him again. I'm having a hard time trying to recall the others' names and faces. The only ones I really remember are Pudgy and Sonia O'Dauyé.

Sonia was the star of the Marivaux Course. She had attended only two or three of the group sessions, since she was taking private lessons with our teacher, a luxury that none of the rest of us could afford. A blonde with a narrow face and very light-colored eyes. She piqued our curiosity from the start. Though only twenty-three, she seemed a good ten or twenty years older than us. She claimed that her family was Polish aristocracy, and to our great surprise, she hadn't been in the course more than a month before she was being mentioned in a magazine of the time. Word was, she would soon be making her "theatrical debut."

Our teacher responded evasively to our questions about the "Countess" — or so we had nicknamed her — and this promising "debut." But Pudgy, who had a bit more street smarts than the rest of us and already frequented the world of backstages, studios, and nightspots, told us that the Countess lived in a luxurious apartment on Cours Albert 1er. Pudgy sensed something fishy about this: No doubt about it, the Countess was a kept woman. She spent a fortune at the dressmaker's and the jeweler's. According to Pudgy, she reserved tables for ten at the fanciest restaurants, treated practically anyone to dinner, and handed out gifts like confetti; there were those who gladly accepted. Pudgy, meanwhile, was dying to join the Countess's entourage.

But today, none of this would matter any more than a crown of wilted flowers on a trash can lid if it weren't for Little Jewel.

I met her the day of the annual contest. Our teacher had set up a stage in the living room of her apartment, and among the fifty or so spectators sat a jury, composed of several personalities from the world of arts and entertainment.

I was too recent a student to compete in this ceremony, and

out of shyness I showed up at Rue Beaujon only after the contest had ended. In the "theater," Pudgy and a few others were engaged in lively conversation.

"The Countess took first prize for tragedy," Pudgy told me. "I got honorable mention in variety."

I congratulated him.

"She chose the Lady of the Camellias' death scene, but she blew her lines."

He leaned in closer.

"The whole thing was rigged . . . It's a fix, old man . . . The Countess must have bribed the jury and Madame Sans-Gêne . . ."

Madame Sans-Gêne—"Madame Shameless"—was our teacher's nickname. She had shone in that role, once upon a time.

"Imagine, those photographers came especially for the Countess. She got herself interviewed . . . A regular movie star. She must have paid them all a bundle . . ."

It was at that moment that I noticed, at the very back of the room, a little girl fast asleep on one of the red velvet chairs.

"Who's that?" I asked Pudgy.

"The Countess's daughter. She doesn't seem to have much time for her. She handed her over to me for the afternoon. Except, that's not so great for me. I have an audition to go to . . . You wouldn't mind looking after her for me, would you?"

"Fine by me."

"Just take her out for a bit of a walk and then bring her back to the Countess's, 24 Cours Albert 1er."

"Sure."

"I'm off, then. Can you imagine? They might hire me for a cabaret!"

He was all excited and sweating profusely.

"Break a leg, Pudge."

The only ones left in that makeshift theater were the sleeping little girl and me. I went up to her: her cheek was resting against the back of the chair, her left hand on her shoulder and her arm folded across her chest. She had blond ringlets and was wearing a pale blue coat with heavy brown shoes. She must have been six or seven.

I tapped her softly on the shoulder. She opened her eyes.

Light blue eyes, almost gray, like the Countess.

"We have to go for a walk."

She got up. I took her by the hand and the two of us left the Marivaux Course.

■

Following Avenue Hoche, we had arrived at the fence around the Parc Monceau.

"Shall we go in there?"

"Okay."

She nodded obediently.

To the left, near the boulevard, I spotted swings with peeling paint, an old slide, and a concrete sandbox.

"You want to play?"

"Okay."

Nobody. Not a single child. The sky was overcast and white as cotton wool, as if it were about to snow. She took two or three turns down the slide, then asked me in a timid voice to help her onto the swing. She didn't weigh much. I pushed the swing on which she sat very stiffly. Now and again, she looked back at me.

"What's your name?"

"Martine, but my mommy calls me Jewel."

Someone had left a shovel in the sandbox, and she started making sand pies. Sitting on a nearby bench, I noticed that her socks were of mismatched size and color: one, dark green, stretched to her knee; the other, blue, stuck out only a few inches from the brown shoe with its untied laces. Had the Countess dressed her that day?

I was afraid she might catch cold in the sand, and after tying her shoe I led her to the other side of the park. A few children were spinning on the merry-go-round. She chose a seat in one of the wooden swans, and the merry-go-round started up with a screech. Each time she passed by me, she raised her arm in a wave, a smile on her lips, her left hand clutching the swan's neck.

After five turns, I told her her mom was waiting and we should take the metro back.

"It would be nicer to walk home."

"If you like."

I didn't have the heart to refuse. I wasn't even old enough to be her father.

We headed toward the Seine via Rue Monceau and Avenue George-V. It was the time of day when the building façades still stood out against the slightly lighter sky, but soon everything would blend together in the dark. We had to hurry. As on every evening at that particular hour, I was gripped by a vague anxiety. She was too: I felt the squeeze of her hand in mine.

From the landing outside the apartment, I heard the sounds of conversation and laughter. A brunette of about fifty, with short hair and the square, aggressive face of a bull terrier, opened the door. She looked at me suspiciously.

"Hello, Madeleine-Louis," the little girl said.

"Hi, Jewel."

"I've brought . . . Jewel home," I said.

"Come in."

In the foyer, bouquets of flowers were lying on the floor, and farther in, through the half-open double doors of the living room, I could make out clusters of people.

"Just a moment . . . I'll get Sonia," the woman with the terrier face said to me.

The little girl and I waited together amid the sprays of flowers strewn around the foyer.

"That's a lot of flowers," I said.

"They're for Mom."

The Countess appeared, blonde and glowing, in a black velvet suit with jet-beaded shoulders.

"How kind of you to bring Jewel home."

"Oh, really . . . The least I could do . . . Congratulations . . . on your first prize."

"Thank you . . . Thank you . . ."

I felt awkward and wanted to leave that apartment as quickly as possible.

She turned to her daughter.

"Jewel, today is a big day for your mommy, you know . . ."

The little girl stared at her with disproportionately wide-open eyes. From astonishment or fear?

"Jewel, Mommy got a very nice award today . . . You should give your mommy a kiss . . ."

But as she didn't lean down toward her daughter, the girl, standing on tiptoe, tried to kiss her in vain. The Countess didn't even notice. She stared at the bouquets lying on the floor.

"Jewel, do you realize . . . All those flowers . . . There are so many I'll never be able to put them in vases . . . I have to get back to my friends . . . And take them to dinner . . . I'll be home very late . . . You wouldn't mind watching Jewel tonight, would you?"

Her tone of voice indicated that this was not a question.

"If you like," I said.

"They'll make you some dinner. And you can sleep here."

I didn't have a chance to answer. She bent toward Jewel.

"Good night, Jewel darling . . . I have to go see my friends . . . Keep Mommy in your thoughts."

She gave her a fleeting kiss on the forehead.

"And thank you again, Monsieur . . ."

With a nimble stride, she went to join the others in the living room. Amid the buzz of conversation, I thought I made out the shrill sound of her laughter.

Gradually their voices faded as they made their way down the stairs, and once more I found myself alone with Jewel. She led me to the dining room and we sat facing each other over a long, rectangular table veined to look like marble. My seat was a garden chair stained with rust, and Jewel's a stool with a red velvet cushion for added height. No other furniture in the room. Light fell on us from a wall lamp with bare bulbs.

A Chinese cook served us dinner.

"Is he nice?" I asked.

"Yes."

"What's his name?"

"Chung."

She ate her soup conscientiously, her torso rigid.

She remained silent throughout the meal.

"May I get up from the table?"

"You may."

She showed me her room, which had sky-blue woodwork. The only furnishings were a child's bed and, between the two windows, a round table covered with a satin cloth on which stood a lamp.

She slipped into the bathroom next door and I heard her brushing her teeth. When she came back, she was wearing a white nightshirt.

"Can I have a drink of water please?"

She had said it very fast, as if apologizing in advance.

"Of course."

I went wandering in search of the kitchen, guided by a flashlight Jewel had lent me. I pictured her, holding that flashlight that was too heavy for her, alone at night, terrified by the shadows around her. Most of the rooms were empty. I tried turning on the lights as I passed by, but often the switches didn't work. The apartment looked abandoned. On the walls, rectangular discolorations showed where paintings used to hang. In a room that must have been the Countess's, a large bed with padded white satin posts had pride of place. A telephone on the floor and, around the bed, bunches of red roses, a powder compact, a scarf.

I'm not sure why, but I went rummaging through the chest of drawers and came across an old brown sheet of paper with the name and address of Odette Blache, 15 Quai du Point-du-Jour, Boulogne-sur-Seine. At the bottom were two photos, one frontal, the other in profile. I easily recognized the Countess, but she was younger, wearing a blank expression as if they were anthropometric photos.

At the kitchen table, the Chinese cook was playing cards with another Chinese man and a redhead with pale skin.

"I've come to fetch the little girl a glass of water."

He pointed to the sink. I filled the glass and glanced over at them. Scattered on the wax tablecloth were food ration cards. That was the ante. The door shut slowly behind me. The closer mechanism creaked.

Again the succession of empty rooms, from which the furniture had no doubt been hastily removed not long before. To what storage place? And the white satin bed, the two chairs piled high with trunks and valises, the solitary couch against the wall bespoke a temporary setup.

She was waiting for me in her bed.

"Can you read me a story?"

Once more she seemed to be apologizing as she handed me a book with a tatty cover: *The Prisoner of Zenda.* Strange reading for a little girl. She listened, arms folded, an expression of delight in her eyes.

When the chapter was over, she asked me not to turn off the light, nor the chandelier in the next room. She was afraid of the dark. I poked my head through the door to see whether she was asleep. And then I wandered through the apartment, finally coming across a leather armchair in which to spend the night.

■

The next day, the Countess offered me a job as tutor. Her social and artistic obligations would no longer permit her to look after Jewel. She was counting on my help. Without much regret I abandoned the Marivaux Course, in which I had enrolled mainly to combat my loneliness. Now that someone was giving me responsibilities and offering me bed and board, I felt much more sure of myself.

I brought Jewel to a Swiss matron who gave private lessons at the Kulm School on Rue Jean-Goujon. Jewel seemed to be the only pupil at this institution, and whenever I went to pick her up, morning and afternoon, I always found her with that woman, in the back of a classroom as dark and silent as a disused chapel. The rest of the day was spent at the edge of the lawn on Cours Albert 1er or in the gardens at Trocadéro. And we walked back home along the river.

Yes, all of that was framed by winter and night as if in a velvet box. It wasn't only the darkness Jewel was afraid of, but also the shadows projected onto her curtains by the lamp in her room and, through the half-open doorway, the chandelier in the adjoining room.

She saw threatening hands in them and huddled in her bed. I murmured soothing words until she fell asleep. I tried every way I could to dissipate those shadows.

The simplest thing would have been to open the curtains, but the lamplight threatened to alert the air raid wardens. So I moved the lamp around, to the right, to the left: the shadows remained.

My presence calmed her. After about two weeks, she had forgotten about the hands on the curtains and would fall asleep before I finished reading the nightly chapter of *The Prisoner of Zenda.*

It snowed heavily that winter, and the neighborhood we lived in—Cours Albert 1er, the terrace of the modern art museum, and farther on the tiered streets on the flank of the Passy slope—

looked like the ski resort at Engadine. Around Place de la Concorde, the King of the Belgians astride his horse was as white as if he'd just ridden through a blizzard. I'd found Jewel a toboggan in a junk shop, and I took her sledding down a gently sloping path in the Trocadéro gardens. In the evenings, returning via Avenue de Tokyo, I dragged the toboggan with Jewel seated on it, rigid and daydreaming as usual. I stopped short. We pretended we were lost in a forest. The idea made her laugh, and her cheeks flushed.

At around 7 p.m., the Countess barely took the time to kiss her daughter before vanishing to some nighttime fête. The mysterious Madeleine-Louis with her boxer's face spent all afternoon on the phone without paying us any mind. What business was that woman transacting? In a harsh voice, she made appointments at her "office," for which she gave an address in the Arcades du Lido. Apparently she exerted a huge influence over the Countess, whom she called not Sonia but Odette, and I wondered if she wasn't where the "money came from," as Pudgy put it. Did she live at Cours Albert 1er? Several times I'd had the impression that she and Sonia came home together at dawn, but I believe Madeleine-Louis often slept in her "office."

Recently, she had acquired a houseboat, moored near the Ile de Puteaux, where we had visited her one Sunday, Jewel, the Countess, and I. She had fixed up a living room in it, with sofas and cushions to sit on. That day, her sailor's cap and white bell-bottoms made her look like a fat, ominous midshipman.

She served tea. I recall that on one of the teakwood walls

hung the photo of a friend of hers in a red frame, a chanteuse with bobbed hair, a descendant of Robert Surcouf; her songs were about ports of call, pale-colored sloops, and rain-soaked harbors.

Was it under her sway that Madeleine-Louis had purchased the houseboat?

When evening fell, Madeleine-Louis and the Countess left Jewel and me in the living room. I helped her with a jigsaw puzzle that I'd chosen myself, its pieces large enough not to be too difficult for her.

The Seine was flooded that winter and the water rose almost to the portholes, fresh water whose odor of mud and lilacs filled the room.

The two of us navigated a scape of marshlands. The farther up the river we traveled, the more I gradually reverted to her age. We drifted past the coast of Boulogne, near where I was born, between the Bois and the Seine . . .

And that man, the one of about thirty, whom I would hear walking around two or three times a week, at night, when I was alone with Jewel . . . He had a key to the apartment and often came in through the service entrance. The first time, he introduced himself as "Jean Bori," Sonia's "brother"—but then, why didn't they share the same last name?

Madeleine-Louis had confided to me, in a smarmy voice, that the O'Dauyés—Sonia's family—were Irish nobility who had settled in Poland in the eighteenth century. And for that matter, why was Sonia also called Odette?

This Jean Bori, Sonia's brother, with his thin face and pock-marked skin, seemed pleasant enough. When he arrived earlier than usual and did not have the Chinese cook serve him his dinner alone, the three of us would eat together, he, Jewel, and I. He showed the little girl an absentminded affection. Her father? He was always nicely dressed, with a tie pin. Where did he sleep at Cours Albert 1er? In Sonia's room or on a couch in some lost corner of the apartment?

Normally he left late, clutching an envelope that bore the words "For Jean" in Sonia's large handwriting. He avoided Madeleine-Louis and visited when she wasn't there.

One evening, he wanted to stay for Jewel's bedtime and sat at the foot of the bed to listen to the nightly reading from *The Prisoner of Zenda*. We each gave Jewel a good-night kiss.

In the large, dreary room we called the salon, the Chinese cook served us two cognacs.

"Odette is really something else . . ."

He took a dog-eared photo from his wallet and handed it to me.

"That was when Odette was first starting out, five years ago. She got spotted by some bigwig that evening . . . Nice picture, don't you think?"

Tables with white cloths. And around those tables, a large gathering of people in formal wear. An orchestra on a bandstand, way in back. The bright spotlights lit an alpine décor composed of three small chalets, a pine tree; the cardboard mountains were covered in fake snow, like the roofs of the chalets and the branches of the pine tree. Opposite the diners in their tuxedos and evening gowns, some thirty mountain infantrymen, in two rows, stood at attention, their feet in skis. The floor, too, glistened with fake snow, and I didn't dare ask Jean Bori whether those mountain infantrymen had remained there, immobile on their skis, until the end of the evening, and what had been Odette's exact role in all this. Program vendor?

"It was a gala . . . The 'Ski Ball' . . ."

For me, that ersatz snow and winter that had marked Odette's "debut" blended with reality. You only had to lean out the window and contemplate the snow on Cours Albert 1er.

"Is Odette paying you enough to work as a governess?"

"Yes."

He looked pensive.

"It's nice of you to take such good care of the kid . . ."

Showing him out to the landing, I couldn't help asking whether he and his sister really belonged to a family of Irish nobility that had emigrated to Poland in the eighteenth century. He appeared not to understand.

"Who, us—Polish? Did Odette tell you that?"

He put on his parka.

"Yeah, sure, we're Polish . . . Polish straight out of Porte-Dorée."

His laughter echoed in the stairwell while I stood frozen in the middle of the foyer.

I walked through the empty apartment. Pockets of darkness. Rolled-up carpets. The outlines on the walls of missing paintings and furniture and bare floors, as if everything had been repossessed. And the two Chinese men were surely playing cards in the kitchen.

She was asleep, her cheek on the pillow. A sleeping child, and someone to watch over her — that's still something, amid all the emptiness.

The whole thing fell apart because of an idea of Madeleine-Louis's that Sonia thought was brilliant: Jewel should work "in show business." If they really took her in hand, she would soon be the equal of that American child star. Sonia seemed to have given up on any sort of artistic career for herself, and I wonder whether she and Madeleine-Louis weren't projecting their frustrated dreams onto Jewel.

I explained to the director of the Kulm School on Rue Jean-Goujon that Jewel would no longer be attending classes there. She was very sorry about losing her only pupil, as was I, for her sake and for Jewel's.

We had to create a wardrobe for her, in preparation for the photos to send to the production companies. They made her a horse riding outfit, a skating outfit like Sonja Henie's, and one for a model little girl. Her mother and Madeleine-Louis brought her to endless fittings, and from the window I watched Sonia's buggy leave Cours Albert 1er in the snow, its black top folded down. I felt a pang in my heart. The little girl was squeezed between her mother and Madeleine-Louis, and the latter cracked a whip over the horse, like a circus tamer.

My job was to take her to her lessons. Piano lessons. Dance lessons. Elocution lessons with our teacher from Rue Beaujon. Photo sessions in a studio on Avenue d'Iéna, in her various costumes. Riding lessons at a bridle school in the Bois de Boulogne. For those, at least, she was outdoors and got some color back, so small, so blonde, on a dapple gray horse that blended in with the snow and morning fog.

She never said a word and always showed complete obedience, despite her exhaustion. One afternoon when Madeleine-Louis and Sonia had granted her a break, we went to the Trocadéro gardens, and she fell asleep on her sled.

Before long, I had to leave for the South of France. Paris had become dangerous, and I was no longer sure I could rely on the identity card I'd been given by an old friend from Valvert. Jewel's name wasn't really Jewel, Sonia's wasn't Sonia, and I wasn't really called Lenormand.

I asked them to let me bring Jewel, who would surely be happier in the South. In vain. Fat, hard Madeleine-Louis was stuck on her idea of making Jewel a child star. And Sonia . . . She was so suggestible, so evanescent. With her constant habit of listening to the "Moonlight Sonata" and staring into space . . . Still, I always suspected that beneath her tulles and vapors lurked the toughness of a fishwife.

I left early one morning, before the girl woke up.

A few months later, in Nice, I came across a picture of her on the arts page of a weekly magazine. She had a part in a film called *Archer's Crossing*. She was standing, in her nightgown, holding a flashlight, her face a bit leaner, looking as if she were searching for someone in the empty apartment on Cours Albert 1er.

Me, perhaps.

I never heard from her again. So many winters have passed since then that I don't dare count them.

Pudgy made out fine. He had the flexibility and bounce-back of a rubber ball. But she? The Kulm School on Rue Jean-Goujon, where I used to pick her up mornings and afternoons, no longer exists. When I walk along the river, I remember the snow from those days, which coated the statues of Albert I, King of the Belgians, and of Simón Bolívar, symmetrically placed at a hundred yards' distance. They, at least, haven't budged, each one stiff as ever on his horse, indifferent to the swirls in the murky water that the houseboats leave in their wake.

VI.

It was always in the dining hall, after mail call, that Pedro would announce a student's expulsion. The guilty party had his last meal with us, doing his best to save face, either acting cocky or fighting back tears. I felt anxious and depressed whenever one of us had to suffer this trial. To me he was like a condemned man, and I would have loved to see Pedro grant a stay of execution at the last moment.

Philippe Yotlande's expulsion had affected me deeply, even though he, like Bourdon and Winegrain, was considerably older than I. When I was entering eighth grade, he was repeating eleventh. Our principal had appointed him "cadet" for the Nursery.

As was customary, Pedro served notice of his sentence in the dining hall. Yotlande had chosen to take it lightly and cracked jokes with his tablemates throughout the meal.

At the start of the afternoon, our "cadets" made us walk in quickstep from the Swiss Yard up to the Castle patio. Pedro and the entire faculty, standing on the porch, waited for the noise to die down. Then our principal pronounced the ritual sentence, in a grave, staccato voice:

"Your classmate, Philippe Yotlande, has been expelled."

He and the other teachers stood at attention.

"Philippe Yotlande, will you leave the ranks and come up here . . ."

Yotlande left his friends from eleventh grade and jogged up the porch steps. He had donned his blazer with the school crest that we were expected to put on for dinner every evening.

"Philippe Yotlande, stand at attention facing your schoolmates . . ."

He stood immobile on the porch as if on a scaffold, wearing a shy smile and an apologetic expression.

"Philippe Yotlande, you have been deemed unworthy to remain among us. I hereby expel you from Valvert."

Before going back down the steps, Yotlande held out his hand to Pedro and all the teachers, with such good grace that not a single one of them refused to shake it.

Many years later, one evening at around seven, at the exit of the Paris Racing Club, I spotted Philippe Yotlande from afar, without having the courage to go up to him. Would he still remember Valvert? I didn't need to talk to him. I could guess his frame of mind . . .

Arms resting on the steering wheel, chin on the back of his hand, he sat pensively for a long while in the old convertible that he'd never wanted to give up. It would have been like amputating a part of himself, for that car was linked to a whole period of his life.

What should he do with himself this evening? Every morning was spent at the Racing Club, by the pool. Then he had a pan bagnat and tomato juice at the bar, where he watched the stages of the Tour de France on TV. And then he went back to poolside.

He hadn't spoken to a soul since early in the month, and that suited him fine. Two or three times, at the Club, he had dodged a familiar silhouette. He was surprised by his antisocial behavior, as he had always been so outgoing.

The only time he felt a hint of anxiety was around seven. The prospect of an entire evening and dinner with just himself for company made him nervous, but his nerves settled as he crossed the Bois de Boulogne. The summer air was mild and the park brought back so many memories. There, at the Pré Catalan, he had attended several wedding receptions. Over time his friends had all gotten married.

Farther on, near Neuilly, the bowling alley at the Jardin d'Acclimatation amusement park had been the "in" place, back when Yotlande used to play hooky from a cram school after he'd been expelled from Valvert. He spent almost every afternoon there. You could meet up with the "gangs" from the Molitor or La Muette swimming pools and decide where to hold the next party.

Why had he been thrown out of Valvert? For bringing in a suitcase stuffed to the gills with American blue jeans and records that he sold to the other students at half-price. A friend from the Molitor Pool crowd supplied the goods, which came directly from the PX, where only U.S. Army personnel could shop.

PX: those two letters with their prestigious aura, that inaccessible store that had set the boys of Philippe Yotlande's generation dreaming, would mean nothing to a twenty-year-old today.

PX had been shoved in the attic, along with other old accessories like the ID bracelet on which he'd insisted they engrave "Jean-Philippe": a double first name was more stylish.

At Porte de la Muette, he turned left onto Boulevard Suchet. He drove down it every evening to Porte d'Auteuil, then back up Boulevard Suchet to Porte de la Muette; then he took Boulevard Lannes, arrived at Porte Maillot, made an about-face toward Porte d'Auteuil, and hoped that by the end of this aimless ramble he would have picked a spot to have dinner. But he couldn't make up his mind, and he continued to wander for a long while, very slowly, through the streets of the 16th arrondissement.

At eighteen, he had been the little prince of this neighborhood. In his room in the apartment on Rue Oswaldo-Cruz, he straightened his tie in the mirror one last time, or smoothed his hair against his forehead, or sometimes kept it brushed back with a dab of clear makeup. He often wore a blazer and gray slacks, the jacket emblazoned with the crest of the Motor Yacht Club on the French Riviera, where his father was a member; and for footwear, Italian loafers with a small coin in each slot—very fashionable back then. Some even used a gold louis.

Stuck in the mirror frame were invitation cards for Saturday evening. Engraved on those white cards were compact upper-crust names sporting nobiliary particles or hyphens. The parents invited their daughters' friends to what they called a "soiree." Every Saturday evening, Philippe Yotlande hesitated among a dozen such soirees. He chose two or three, aware that his presence would lend them extra cachet. Indeed, a soiree attended by Philippe Yotlande was livelier, more successful than the others. And so he had been among the most sought-after guests at hundreds of soirees.

Soirees in the affluent precincts of Auteuil and Passy, given by a dapper bourgeoisie and minor nobility that frequented the beaches of La Baule or Arcachon. More obscure soirees in the Ecole Militaire neighborhood: the father, colonel or functionary, had stretched his budget so that his daughter could invite her well-heeled girlfriends from the Lycée Victor-Duruy; the atmosphere was a bit dour, the parents present throughout the evening, and they served orangeade. In the 17th arrondissement, staid but convivial soirees thrown by prominent lawyers, whose families summered in Cabourg and wintered in Chamonix. More spectacular soirees at La Muette and Avenue Foch, where the offspring of Protestant, Catholic, and Jewish banks hobnobbed with the most prominent coats of arms of the French aristocracy and several exotic names with Chilean or Argentine inflections. But the evenings Yotlande enjoyed most, and upon which the other parents looked askance for their whiff of scandal and "nouveau riche" taint, were the ones given by the son and two daughters of a corporate lawyer married to a former model, in one of those apartments with balconies in the first addresses on Boulevard Suchet.

A nucleus had formed on Boulevard Suchet, a clique of about a dozen boys and girls, a number of whom had sports cars and, like Yotlande, had been students at the Valvert School. The corporate lawyer's son had received an Aston Martin for his eighteenth birthday; Yotlande made do with a red MG convertible; another drove a pale green Nash . . .

The mistress of the house, the ex-model, sometimes joined in her daughter's parties, as if they were the same age. And one of Philippe Yotlande's most dazzling memories was of that June night when everyone was dancing on the terrace and his friends' mother had started flirting with him. Today she must be getting on in years, but at the time she looked no more than thirty. Freckles on her face and shoulders. That night, between her and him, the flirtation had "gone pretty far"—to use an expression that doesn't mean much anymore.

There were hundreds and hundreds of such evenings. You danced or went off to a quiet corner of the terrace for a few hands of poker, or two of you hid out in a bedroom, like Yotlande and one of the family daughters. You let your mind wander to the strains of Miles Davis, watching the leaves flutter on the trees in the Bois de Boulogne. That happy time in Philippe Yotlande's life had been cut short by his military service.

They sent him to Algeria, two months before the Evian Accords. Then he stayed for a while in Val-de-Grâce hospital and, thanks to the intercession of a friend of his father's, he finished his military career as driver to a naval officer, a good-looking man who was close friends with the maréchal de Lattre. With that officer, Yotlande went on long excursions through the forest.

He had just returned to civilian life when his father passed away. His mother bravely took over Maurice Yotlande Pharmaceutical Laboratories, and since Philippe was old enough to work, they put him in charge of "public relations" for the family firm. He didn't exactly shine, but they turned a blind eye, out of respect for the late, lamented Dr. Yotlande. Several years later, his mother retired to the Midi after selling Yotlande Laboratories to a foreign concern, which netted her and her son a huge profit. Since then, Philippe, who had picked up some rudiments of stocks and bonds, tepidly managed their fortune.

He had come to the intersection of Boulevard Suchet and Avenue Ingres. A car passed him, and the driver, jutting his scarlet bulldog face out of the lowered window, cursed at Yotlande, who answered with a bland smile. There had been a time when he'd have sped up and cut the other car off, but he was past the age for such tomfoolery. He halted beneath the trees of Avenue Ingres and turned the knob on the radio. In a metallic voice, an announcer related the final stage of the Tour de France. The trees, the bench, the little green wooden kiosk, and one of the buildings, to the right, took him back twenty years.

It was there, on Avenue Ingres, that he had gone to visit a beautiful Danish woman, famous at the time, named Annette Stroyberg. A photographer for *Paris-Match*, a man much older than Philippe Yotlande who had developed a liking for him, introduced him to a less bourgeois milieu than the one he'd been frequenting. And so he rubbed shoulders with a few cover girls and starlets, at the Belle Ferronnière or the Bar des Théâtres. But his most memorable encounter was with Annette Stroyberg.

He saw Annette a second time the following winter in a

nightspot in Megève, went up to reintroduce himself, and as
luck would have it a flash went off. The photo took up a full page
of a magazine with the caption, "Stars of the screen and Paris
High Society meet for après-ski." There was Philippe Yotlande,
a star sitting with Annette Stroyberg and a dozen other stars. He
was smiling. The photo was passed around at soirees and earned
Yotlande even more prestige. The darling of the 16th arrondissement, photographed in Megève at Annette Stroyberg's side, had
hit his peak at the age of nineteen.

It was after his military service that he slowly began feeling
his age. At the soirees he continued to frequent, he met fewer and
fewer of his contemporaries: work, marriage, and adult life had
claimed them one by one. Yotlande found himself facing kids for
whom the calypso and cha-cha-cha of his adolescence were as
outmoded as the minuet, and who had no idea what the PX was.
He refrained from showing them the Megève picture, which had
yellowed in the five years since, like those photos from the summer of '39 in which you see night owls in Juan-les-Pins dancing
the Chamberlaine.

But he was still basically carefree at heart; he learned the
new dances and preserved his role as life of the party.

She was eighteen and they met at a gathering. She belonged
to a family of Belgian industrialists. The Carton de Borgraves
owned apartments in Paris and Brussels, a chateau in the Ar-
dennes, and a villa in Knokke-le-Zoute. Their daughter seemed
completely smitten with Philippe Yotlande and after a few

months her parents held his feet to the fire: either get engaged or Philippe Yotlande would never see her again.

The engagement ceremony was held in Brussels; that evening, the Carton de Borgraves gave a reception in their home on Avenue Louise. Yotlande had invited all his Paris friends. His future in-laws were taken aback by the eccentricities in which these young French persons indulged, come midnight. One of the corporate lawyer's daughters from Boulevard Suchet, who had had a bit too much champagne, performed a striptease, while another partygoer downed glass after glass to the health of Queen Elizabeth of Belgium, tossing his empties over the balcony.

The family had decided that the fiancés would spend a well-chaperoned holiday at the villa in Zoute, and the Carton de Borgraves invited Philippe Yotlande's mother to join them for the month of August. At first, Yotlande played tennis with his betrothed and some of her friends. Perhaps it was the atmosphere of the villa, the "Castel Borgrave," a huge Tudor-style edifice in which his future mother-in-law, at tea time, detailed for him all her important relations: with the princesse de Rethy, with whom she was on a first-name basis; with the baron Jean Lambert, who couldn't stand the sun. Perhaps it was the gilded—heavily gilded—youth of the place, with their craze for go-kart racing. Or the gaggle of mature men in yachting outfits, who greeted each other on the sidewalks of seaside cafés, laboring to give their gestures a nonchalance worthy of Saint-Tropez. Perhaps it was the leaden sky, or the wind, or the rain. But it was too much for

Philippe Yotlande. After ten days, he skipped out of Zoute by the first train, leaving behind a letter of apology for the girl who had been his fiancée.

Evening fell over Avenue Ingres, and he finally made up his mind to drive on. He followed Boulevard Suchet toward Porte d'Auteuil. The memory of his broken engagement still pained him.

At the time, he had felt a certain relief and returned to his old habits. But at the soirees that he persisted in attending, they made him feel old. Naturally, everyone still loved him. He had become a kind of mascot.

Yes, things had changed. First and foremost, Philippe Yotlande's appearance clashed with his juniors'. Yotlande wore his hair short and still affected the kind of blazer he'd sported at eighteen. He tended toward beige suits with crepe-soled shoes and kept his tan year round. In this, he remained faithful to the model for adolescents of his generation: athletic Americans from the early nineteen fifties.

Time passed. And Philippe Yotlande had to fill his days. He devoted much of his life to tennis and winter sports, and took on the habits of an aging bachelor, spending a month every year at his mother's in Cannes.

His old friends invited him for the holidays, for they knew Yotlande would be pleasant company. Their children loved him. With them, more than with their parents, he rediscovered his former verve, from the time of parties on Chris-Crafts and nights out at the Esquinade.

Gradually, a certain melancholy wormed its way into him. It had begun around the time of his thirty-fifth birthday. And since then, he preferred to remain alone, to "meditate," as he said — something that had never happened to him before . . .

Reaching Porte d'Auteuil, he took the opposite direction back up Boulevard Suchet, to Porte de la Muette. He braked at the top of Avenue Henri-Martin. His wristwatch said eight-thirty, and he still didn't know where to have dinner.

No matter. He had time. He followed Avenue Henri-Martin, then veered left onto Avenue Victor-Hugo. Farther on, at the square, he got out of the car, shutting the door gently behind him, and strolled toward the sidewalk tables of the Café Scossa.

It was there that he ended up every evening at the same time, as if he had slid, without even realizing it, toward a mysterious center of gravity. There are places that act as magnets for disoriented souls, solid boulders in the storm. For Philippe Yotlande, the Scossa was like the final vestige of his youth, the last fixed point in the chaos.

Back when, the sidewalk of the Scossa was where they arranged to meet. Summer evenings, like today, where flirtations developed, in the murmur of the fountains and the leaves on the trees, while the church bell chimed the start of the holidays . . .

He ordered an ice cream soda. Back when he would skip classes at his cram school, he used to go enjoy them with a friend, where they served the best ones: in the Arcades off the Champs-Elysées.

Almost dark. Several cars crossed Place Victor-Hugo. He

looked around him. There were few customers at the sidewalk tables. Inside, in back, he noticed Pam-Pam Mickey and couldn't help staring at his platinum blond pompadour, dazzling under the neon lights: the wave that crested above his forehead and the turbulent, undulating cascade down the back of his neck. Mickey had remained faithful to the hairstyle of his youth.

The great tragedy of Mickey's life had been the closing of the Pam-Pam bar on the Champs-Elysées, at the corner of Rue Lincoln. For more than twenty years he had held court there, having reached his peak during the war, when the "swing kids" frequented the place and Mickey was the most celebrated of them all. His honorific, "Pam-Pam Mickey," dated from that period. After losing his fiefdom, he had wistfully emigrated to the Scossa.

Surreptitiously, Yotlande watched the aged young man of sixty, alone at his table, head bowed under the weight of his peroxide coif. What was Pam-Pam Mickey thinking about this evening? And why do certain people remain prisoners, well into old age, of a single year in their lives, becoming the decrepit caricature of what they used to be in their heyday?

And he, Philippe Yotlande—wouldn't he become another Pam-Pam Mickey in a few years? The prospect gave him chills, but he hadn't lost his jocular nature and, surprised by his absorption in such serious topics, he decided then and there to give himself a future nickname: "Hamlet of the Scossa."

A few tables away, a girl of about twenty was sitting with a gray-haired man, who held his head high and looked like a gentleman rider, with an official decoration on his lapel. Her grandfather, thought Yotlande. The man stood up and walked into the café, leaning on a cane.

The girl remained alone at the table. She was blonde, with bangs and high cheekbones. She was drinking grenadine through a straw.

Yotlande stared at her. She looked like his Belgian ex-fiancée.

What if, taking advantage of her grandfather's momentary absence, he went over to introduce himself and make a date, bowing, as if inviting the woman to dance?

He watched her drink her grenadine. He had turned thirty-eight in June, but still could not entirely reconcile himself to the fact that the world was not an endless party.

VII.

My friend Daniel Desoto was also expelled from school, and I had to find a new partner in the projection booth.

Desoto suffered the same treatment as Yotlande: the announcement of his expulsion in the dining hall, walking up the porch steps in front of the assembled students and silent faculty, Pedro's harsh voice declaring him "unworthy" . . . But his attitude was not like his older classmate's.

A few weeks after his expulsion, he came to visit us behind the wheel of a red sports coupe that he parked right in front of the Castle. It was recess, and we huddled in admiration around the vehicle. Desoto said that his father, whom he called by the English term "Daddy," had given it to him for his birthday. And at our astonishment that he could drive before he was old enough for a license, he explained that Daddy had "arranged" for him to get Belgian nationality: in Belgium, apparently, "you can drive without a license." We'd all known how much Daddy spoiled his son since Desoto had shown us photos of the sailboat Daddy had bought him the summer before.

Our group attracted the attention of Mr. Jeanschmidt, who asked Desoto to vacate the premises at once. He had been expelled because of his cavalier attitude and his spoiled whims, and they didn't wish to see any more of him at Valvert. Without missing a beat, Desoto, smiling, slowly opened the car door, pulled a carton of American cigarettes from the glove compartment, and handed it to Pedro.

"Here, sir, these are for you . . . with Daddy's compliments."

Then he sped away in a screech of tires.

◾

Fifteen years later, passing through a resort on the Atlantic coast, I ran into him on the boardwalk along the seashore. He recognized me immediately. He had lost his chubby cheeks and his brown hair was enlivened by a shock of white.

The next day, he called to invite me to lunch at the local tennis club.

It was a beautiful day. Beneath the large pergola of the tennis club, near the bar, two tables were reserved in the name of "Mr. Desoto."

A man of about sixty, in tennis whites, strode toward me with a limber gait. He held out his hand and smiled. A reptilian smile. Was it due to the sinuous form of his lips?

"Are you here to see Daniel?"

"Yes."

"Doctor Réoyon. I'm a friend of Daniel's."

And with an ecclesiastical gesture, pressing my shoulder, he bade me sit back down.

Why did this Dr. Réoyon inspire such immediate unease?

Things like that can't be explained. He watched me, squinting, a smile floating over his sinuous lips. I looked for something to break the silence.

"Have you known Daniel very long?"

"Yes. Very long. And you?"

His question contained a hint of challenge, as if I represented a threat to him, or he considered me a rival.

Fortunately, Desoto joined us. He was wearing white shorts and a navy blue jacket, and our reunion made us both feel awkward.

"Have you met Doctor Réoyon? He's my best friend," he blurted out. "I owe him practically everything, you know . . ."

"Come now, Daniel, not in the slightest," the doctor exclaimed. "It is I who am honored by your friendship."

Then, turning to me:

"Daniel is married to a marvelous woman. Have you met her?"

"My wife will be here any moment," Daniel said to me, smiling. "Will you have an aperitif?"

And as I hesitated, he turned to the bartender.

"Two Americanos, Michel. And an Orgeat syrup for Doctor Réoyon."

From the way "Michel" snapped to it, one could tell that Desoto was a prominent figure here at the tennis club. We sat down on the white wooden chairs, at one of the tables reserved in the name of Mr. Desoto.

"You know, you have here before you a truly remarkable

man," Desoto said to me, gesturing toward the doctor. "Let me tell you about him . . ."

Réoyon shrugged modestly. A group came toward us, composed of a young blonde and several teenagers in tennis outfits.

"My wife, Gunilla," Desoto said, introducing me to the very beautiful blonde.

She gave me barely a look and a brief nod. Then she smiled at Dr. Réoyon. The latter stood up and kissed her hand with the same gentle insistence he had earlier used to press my shoulder down.

Daniel Desoto ordered crudité salads and rosé wine for us, a raw egg and water for Dr. Réoyon. He seemed to be familiar with the latter's every habit.

Desoto's wife was Swedish. She spoke French in a deep, commanding voice. The three or four teenagers lunching with us bustled around her, but clearly felt equal admiration for Daniel Desoto.

Dr. Réoyon called the teenagers by their first names and showed them the gruff affection of an old scoutmaster bullying his cubs. All anyone talked about during the meal were Daniel Desoto's serves or backhands from that morning, and everyone complimented him on the quality of his smashes. The only criticisms came from Dr. Réoyon, and Desoto listened to him with his mouth slightly agape. What role did the doctor play in my old friend's life? Gunilla Desoto nonchalantly smoked a cigarette and stated that she would be on the courts that afternoon. The teenagers vied to see who would have the honor of being her partner with as much urgency as the Sun King's courtiers jockeying to become the next Marly. Réoyon, in canonical tones, proposed that they draw straws.

Everyone who passed by under the pergola greeted Daniel Desoto, his wife, and Dr. Réoyon. The bartender didn't take his eyes off us and anticipated our every wish. Daniel and Gunilla Desoto were the monarchs of the tennis club, all its members their subjects, and Dr. Réoyon their éminence grise. Evidently Dany was what they generally call in club circles "very well off." And I was proud of my friend to see that he'd married such a gorgeous woman and become a man of consequence.

I knew something about precious stones, and I noticed on Gunilla Desoto's finger a Ural emerald and a diamond of the first water. I raised my eyes, and they met those of Dr. Réoyon. A strange look, the kind a cardsharp gives a newcomer whom he suspects of also playing with a marked deck.

"Beautiful stones, aren't they? I recommended them to Gunilla for their therapeutic virtues," Réoyon said.

"Meaning?" I said.

"Meaning that Doctor Réoyon can cure you of any ailment," Gunilla said curtly.

"It's true, old man," Daniel Desoto chimed in. "And Doctor Réoyon can put you to sleep in a minute flat . . . He just has to massage your forehead . . . Go on, Doctor, show him."

"Don't be childish, Daniel."

The doctor's rimmed and sinuous lips tightened. The hardness on his face froze my blood.

"Forgive me, Doctor . . . I merely wanted to show my friend what you're capable of . . ."

"Medicine is serious business, Daniel."

His unctuous tone had returned.

"Doctor Réoyon is right, darling," Gunilla added to settle the matter.

All afternoon, I remained seated under the pergola. Daniel Desoto had reserved the central court to play tennis. Now and then he made a brief appearance, looking increasingly agitated, reiterating that he "wasn't in tip-top form," despite the constant encouragements his young admirers lavished on him. Gunilla, looking worried, told me in her deep voice that Daniel was restless and always felt the need to exert himself. It was a good thing Dr. Réoyon was watching over him.

At the end of the match, Daniel furiously threw his racket against one of the pillars of the pergola, then went to sulk at the bar, like a child. His entourage must have been used to these outbursts, since none of his courtiers — not even Dr. Réoyon — went to disturb his sulk. Gunilla slipped away, after picking up Daniel's racket and whispering a few words to Dr. Réoyon, who nodded and disappeared in turn.

I tapped Daniel on the shoulder. He turned around and smiled at me, with that kind, slightly melancholy smile that I remembered from our school days. Then he pulled me toward the edge of the pergola, away from the others. We sat on a bench.

"How's Daddy?" I asked.

As it happened, Daddy was still around. At seventy-five, Daddy was still in very good health. And Desoto told me that, in fact, he and his wife spent vacations here, with Daddy and Mammy, as he called his mother. They all stayed at the Belle-vue, the hotel where, every year, since he was a small child, he, Daniel, had sojourned for a month with Daddy and Mammy. The Bellevue, he said, was like their home. And the tennis club his estate. Daddy had enrolled him in it at age three, by special dispensation.

And since we were such old friends, he opened up to me: after a year spent dithering, during which Daniel had "suffered some hard knocks" and worked for a sympathetic friend of his father's, Daddy had finally agreed to let him marry Gunilla, on condition that Gunilla give up her modeling career and convert to Judaism. Daddy had bought them a huge apartment on Rue Jean-Goujon, and Mammy had overseen the decoration. Yes, it was Daddy who had lent him the money to buy Gunilla those rings.

Daddy had entrusted him with a small, undemanding job in his film import-export company. The best part was that they got to travel a lot and never missed Cannes, which Gunilla greatly enjoyed.

And what about Dr. Réoyon in all this? I sensed Daniel hesi-tate. Oh, Dr. Réoyon was a kind of adviser who accompanied them wherever they went. The doctor lived with them on Rue

Jean-Goujon. He and Gunilla owed a lot to Dr. Réoyon. And Daddy—what did he make of this doctor? That time, Daniel didn't answer. He changed the subject by telling me that he and Gunilla wanted a child. In the apartment on Rue Jean-Goujon, the nursery was all ready. A very large, sky-blue nursery. And Daniel confided that he slept there alone. Funny thing, isn't it?

He walked me to the club entrance that marked the border of his realm. He seemed touched when I asked him to remember me fondly to Daddy and Mammy. I crossed over the highway and glanced back. I saw him waving to me, looking eternally downcast, his white forelock plastered over his forehead. That forelock was his only sign of aging, but it seemed hard to believe, for it was so white that the hair appeared bleached.

■

Someone gently squeezed my shoulder. I turned around. Doctor Réoyon.

"I'd like to speak with you," he said in a flat voice.

Under his arm was a thin leather portfolio whose color clashed with the immaculate white of his tennis outfit. How did he happen to be there? Had he followed Daniel and me when we left the club? Or had he stationed himself across the road to wait for me?

"This way, please . . ."

We soon came to a mini-golf course, its grounds protected from the highway by white wooden fences and privet hedges. A blonde woman was working behind the counter, in a rustic-style cabin with a thatched roof.

"Will you be playing, Doctor?"

And already she was tendering a golf club.

"No, no, we're just here for drinks."

He signaled for me to sit at one of the tables.

"Two Orgeats . . ."

"Very good, Doctor."

He had laid his portfolio flat on the table and was caressing the leather with the tips of his fingers.

"I would rather you not see Daniel again," he said tersely.

"Why's that?"

"Because I don't believe it's good for him."

He transfixed me with his serpentine gaze. No doubt he was trying to intimidate me. But in reality, I felt like laughing.

"How could I do him any harm? We've been friends since childhood . . ."

"You've just said the magic word."

His tone had softened. Once more there was that unctuous, plummy way of speaking. And he kept caressing the leather of his portfolio. His hand ran back and forth and an image flashed across my mind, with the power and precision of an unassailable fact: I saw that hand gently caressing Gunilla Desoto's buttocks.

"You get along well with Daniel's wife?" I asked him point blank.

"Very well. Why?"

"Just asking . . ."

"A moment ago, you said a key word," Réoyon resumed nervously. "The word *childhood*. Daniel has remained a child. That's the whole problem . . ."

He slowly took a gulp of Orgeat, then smacked his lips like a wine taster sampling a new vintage.

"And with children, a certain conduct must be observed. It requires a great deal of authority. That's where I come in . . . Daniel's parents are too weak and too old. I am the only one who can solve the problem. With his wife's full consent, of course."

Now, with his index finger, he was caressing the portfolio's zipper.

"If I'd rather you not see Daniel again, it's for his own good . . . Anything that reminds him of his childhood or the boarding school can only worsen his case. I am very sorry to tell you that you would have a deleterious effect on him. Leave him be."

He was certainly not appreciating my smile.

"The situation is much more serious than you realize . . . Daniel's parents understand this perfectly well and have given me carte blanche . . . I have here all the documentation to prove it."

He opened the zipper of his portfolio with the slowness and delicacy one might apply to separating two petals of a flower.

"Would you like to see these documents?"

"No need."

I moved my face closer to his, keeping the smile on my lips, no doubt a threatening smile.

"I am Daniel's guardian . . . His legal guardian," murmured Réoyon.

"And what does his wife make of all this?" I asked.

"She wholeheartedly approves. She even helps me in my work."

He got up and stood stiffly in front of me, in his tennis whites, brown leather portfolio under his arm. From the hedgerows came whiffs of privet as strong as in the labyrinth at Valvert.

"Now if you'll excuse me," he said. "Mme Desoto is waiting for her massage."

VIII.

Every year in the month of June, the school festival brought together our parents and friends. They called it the Sports Festival, and those two words in and of themselves express the particular spirit of our school, where sports took primacy. The school badge sewn to our blazers, gold triangle on a blue background, featured the word SPORTS at the base of the triangle like a motto or command.

Kovnovitsyn was in his glory on those Sundays. I can still see him, head held high, wearing a polo shirt, espadrilles, and white trousers, presiding over the ceremony as the marquis de Cuevas once did over his ballets. Shoura, his Labrador, was allowed to walk around off leash for the occasion. And we, the students, vied to outdo each other in the competitive events: hundred-meter dash, athletic exercises, timed run through the fitness trail, pole vaulting. The festival ended at dusk with a game of field hockey, which Pedro himself refereed.

The stars of the day were indisputably the pole vaulters. The best one received a cup from Kovnovitsyn's own hand. But that year, I paid much less attention to my classmates' exploits than to Yvon's sister, Martine.

She was stretched out in a bathing suit on the grass by the

pool. The day's heroes were clustered around her: older boys like Christian Winegrain and Bourdon, the big winners of the pole-vaulting contests, Philippe Yotlande, McFowles, Charell, and others besides . . . Yvon had introduced his sister to all of them and remained at her side, shy and serious like an interpreter or squire. And proud of the success Martine was enjoying.

And I, too, seeing how they all labored to shine around her, felt a certain pride. No other girl, I was convinced, had such auburn hair or light-colored eyes, such a turned-up nose, such long thighs and graceful movements of her bust when she turned to light her cigarette on the lighter that Winegrain held out for her. She was my childhood friend.

She and her brother lived in town, in an ivy-covered house on Rue du Docteur-Dordaine, and Yvon attended the school as a day student. We envied him for being able to go home every evening. His father owned a nursery. The greenhouses behind their home were where we played hide-and-seek: I had lived in that town for three years and met Yvon and his sister at the Jeanne d'Arc School. She, Yvon, and I were the same age—nine or ten at the time—but it seemed to me that Martine was as tall even back then as she was now, beside the pool. It was she who made us our after-school snacks and took us for walks up to the hamlet of Les Metz; she who decided whether we'd play hide-and-seek or fly kites.

My only advantage over the others was that I'd known Martine much longer than they had.

In her honor, Winegrain and Bourdon performed increasingly spectacular dives: the first did a swan dive, the second a jackknife, after walking on his hands up to the pool's edge. For the sports festival, they had poured a little too much methylene blue into the water, and when Winegrain and Bourdon came back to sit with us, their arms and legs looked like they were streaked with ink.

A man of about forty had joined our group. Was he an alumnus or simply someone Yotlande and Winegrain had met during one of the many Paris parties at which they shone?

He, too, seemed captivated by Martine. He couldn't take his eyes off her. Earlier, he had introduced himself in a reedy voice: "Da Silva"—and as he had alluded to an upcoming trip to São Paulo, I had assumed he was Brazilian. He spoke French without the slightest accent. Why did Winegrain, Bourdon, and Yotlande address him familiarly as "Baby"? Was it because of his moon face? His curly brown locks? His almost imperceptible lisp?

"Are you . . . a student at this school?" he asked Martine.

Winegrain guffawed.

"Her? At Valvert? Poor Baby . . ."

Then, turning to Martine:

"You'll have to forgive him, he doesn't know . . . In Brazil . . ."

"Are you really Brazilian?" Martine asked. Her sudden interest in Baby da Silva worried Yvon and me.

"Smart of you to ask," said Winegrain. "For as long as I've known Baby, I've had my doubts."

"Don't listen to them, miss," said Baby in his reedy voice. "I *am* Brazilian, and if you're a nice girl, I'll show you my passport."

She did not watch the hockey game, even though Winegrain and Bourdon begged her to stay, insisting that her presence was necessary. She could not be swayed. In her light blue dress, she headed toward the school gates, walking just as lazily as on those Thursday afternoons when she, Yvon, and I would gather chestnuts in the woods.

Winegrain tried to grab her arm, but she shook him off with a laugh.

"Wouldn't you like to play newlyweds?" he asked her.

"I have no desire to marry you."

"So who do you want to marry, then?" asked Bourdon.

"The richest one," said Martine.

The richest one was surely Winegrain, whom we had nicknamed "Investment Bank, Jr.," or McFowles, whose American grandmother had created the Harriet Strauss cosmetics line.

"You know, they're all rich," Yvon said in a sorrowful voice.

"I'd say the richest one of all has to be Baby," said Winegrain. "Isn't that right, Baby?"

Baby shrugged.

"Don't forget, miss, that I promised to show you my passport," he said with an insinuating smile.

"I'm counting on it . . ."

What sort of look was she giving this Baby da Silva? Sarcastic? Interested? Or both at once?

She left without saying good-bye, as if bored with our company. She abandoned us, passed through the school gates, crossed the small bridge over the Bièvre. And we remained behind the fence, gazing after the tender smudge that her dress made on the twilight.

◾

From then on, they came to collect her every Saturday in a Lancia or a large English car that da Silva drove. First he stopped at the school to pick up Winegrain, Bourdon, and two or three others who squeezed into the back seat. Baby braked sharply in front of the house on Rue du Docteur-Dordaine and honked several times. Martine kissed Yvon and me good-bye, her mind already elsewhere. She ran to the car and it roared off down the tree-lined avenue that led to the highway.

As for me, I stayed home with Yvon. He no longer felt like going into Paris, as he used to do with his sister on Saturday afternoons. On those days, I would meet them at Montparnasse station. We would see a movie, or else Martine dragged us into the shops. In the summer, we would go for a stroll in the Bois de Boulogne and have sandwiches for dinner at an outdoor café. I would walk them back to Montparnasse in time for the last train.

Now, without Martine, the afternoons seemed empty, and we felt jealous of Winegrain, Bourdon, Yotlande, and the other members of the gang whose muse she had become. They looked down on Yvon and me because of our age. They were all nineteen or twenty years old, despite still being tenth- and eleventh-graders.

As for Baby da Silva, what part did he play in all this, exactly?

She would come home at around ten in the evening, and I was still with Yvon, in his room or in the garden. She tried to be as quiet as possible, but we heard the furtive glide of her steps. She never wanted to tell us how she had spent her day. Now and then, she confided that the others had taken her to the movies or a party. She questioned us in turn. She seemed a bit ashamed at having left us all alone on a Saturday, and one evening, no doubt to demonstrate how independent she still was, she told us that Winegrain had tried to give her a gold lighter with black lacquer trim, but she had refused the gift. She had also refused McFowles's present of a Harriet Strauss Beauty Case in blue crocodile.

Winegrain had apparently asked to whom she would "grant her favors." She had answered that she wasn't intending to "grant" them to anyone.

We tried, Yvon and I, to find out more at school, by listening in on conversations among members of the gang. But whenever they saw us, they would lower their voices and snicker, as if they knew something about Martine that we could never suspect.

One day, during recess on the lawn, Winegrain told Yvon and me in a sour voice that Martine had "a thing" for Baby da Silva.

■

And in fact, it was now Baby, and he alone, who came to pick her up every Saturday on Rue du Docteur-Dordaine. Yvon had asked his sister whether the two of us could come with her, but she had sharply refused. Then, realizing she had hurt our feelings, she said:

"I'll ask him for next time."

But she must never have asked, and we didn't dare remind her of her promise.

She watched for the Lancia at the window of Yvon's room. Already she was no longer with us. Her new dress and high-heeled shoes made her look older. She had put on makeup.

He didn't need to honk. Barely had the Lancia stopped in front of the house than Martine was already tripping down the stairs. He opened the door and she leapt into the car beside him. He sped off, and all that haste struck Yvon and me as rather suspect.

■

As the weeks went by, he brought her home later and later. First at ten o'clock, then eleven, then midnight. Yvon and I waited up.

One Saturday we waited until two in the morning. Yvon's parents were away on Saturdays and Sundays. There was an old aunt living in the cottage behind the house who prepared our meals and looked after us, but she went to bed very early.

We began to get worried, and Yvon wanted to call Winegrain or Bourdon, but we didn't have the address or phone number of any members of the gang. Was that Baby da Silva listed in the phone book? Did he live in Paris? When we asked, Martine never answered. And yet, she must have known his address.

We heard the sound of an engine growing more and more distinct in the silence. The Lancia appeared at the bottom of the tree-lined avenue. Its gray body shone in the moonlight. Yvon switched off the lamp in his room so they wouldn't see us at the window. The Lancia came slowly up the hill. It braked in front of the house, but the engine kept running. A door slamming. Peals of laughter. Da Silva's thin voice. At the window, Yvon and I held our breath. Martine leaned into the car and kissed Baby. The latter, before driving off, made his engine roar loudly, as was his habit. His peculiar habit. Martine, standing motionless at the curb, waited until the car had turned the corner of the avenue.

She slammed the front door behind her, and on the stairs her steps were heavier than usual. The sound of someone falling. Her laughter. Was she drunk?

She pushed open Yvon's door. Her silhouette stood out in the frame, against the light from the hall.

"What are you two doing in the dark?"

She turned on the lights and looked at us, one then the other, curiously. Then she again burst out laughing.

"We were waiting for you," said Yvon.

"Now *that's* a good idea."

Her cheeks were flushed, her eyes shining. I felt certain that if we touched her, an electric shock would course through us. Her hair, pale eyes, red mouth, and skin looked phosphorescent.

"I have some big news to tell you."

We were both sitting on the floor, leaning against Yvon's bed.

"Don't just sit there like that . . . You look like you're at a funeral."

"Did you have a good time?" Yvon asked in a dry voice.

"Yes, wonderful. But I have something really important to tell you . . . Let's go down to the living room . . ."

She pulled us up by the arms, laughing. Mixed with her perfume was a slight smell of alcohol, and I wondered whether it was cognac or rum.

■

In the living room, she went to the liquor cabinet and opened it.

"Let's all have a drink, okay?"

She picked up a decanter containing a garnet-colored liquid, on which a small chain held a heart-shaped silver tag.

She poured liquor into the glasses.

"Now, let's toast!"

We toasted. It was the first time we'd drunk alcohol in that living room, and Yvon and I felt a bit embarrassed, as if we were committing sacrilege and our presence there was a transgression.

She let herself drop into one of the armchairs.

"So, here's the thing! I've decided to get married," Martine said in one breath.

Yvon gaped at her, eyes wide. An expression of terror flitted through his eyes.

"You're getting *married?*"

She squeezed the silver tag from the liquor decanter between her fingers, then slipped the chain onto her wrist.

"So you're just leaving us behind?"

Now it was she who stared at her brother in stupefaction. The silver tag slid off her wrist.

"Leaving you behind? What's that supposed to mean?"

"So who are you getting married to?" Yvon insisted.

"Why, Baby . . . Baby da Silva . . ."

The nickname made me want to laugh. A nervous laugh. Baby.

"The Brazilian?"

"Yes . . . He's very sweet, you know . . . I'm sure you'll get along with him."

"But maybe you don't have to get married," Yvon said in a timid voice.

There was a moment of silence. I wished I could have intervened. I tried to find the words to say that, all things considered, marriage was pointless. But I didn't dare open my mouth.

"Yes, yes, I'm going to get married."

Her tone was abrupt, brooking no argument. We each sat stiffly in our chairs.

"Anyway, I don't see how that will change things," said Martine. "Everything will be just as it was. Here, look . . . He's given me an engagement ring."

She held out her hand for us to admire the ring. I was quite young at the time, but I knew something about precious stones. This one was a superb blue-white diamond mounted in platinum.

She leaned toward us.

"Baby is very rich. He has these huge properties in Brazil. I'll tell him we can't be apart. You can come and live with us. Besides, he's willing to do whatever I say . . ."

But it lacked conviction. Something was reaching its end. I looked around me. I knew every stick of furniture, every nook and cranny of this room. It was here that we used to play after our strolls through the woods, here that we celebrated Yvon's and Martine's birthdays. A few Christmases as well. The pine tree in front of the rounded bay window. There was a photo on the cabinet, in a leather frame: Yvon and me wearing short pants and Martine, leaning against a tree, biting into an apple.

"A millionaire . . . Baby is a millionaire, do you realize?" Martine repeated. "Anyway, I'll ask him to buy you a house in Brazil . . ."

She hadn't removed her coat. I thought to myself, this was the last time we'd all be in this room together.

■

I will always remember that building on Rue des Belles-Feuilles, in the part of the street that connects with the Rond-Point

Bugeaud. Winegrain had phoned Yvon at around five o'clock that Saturday afternoon to say that "they" were celebrating Martine's and Baby da Silva's engagement and that our presence was requested.

We took the train, then at Montparnasse we switched to the metro up to Porte Dauphine. The building was, as Winegrain had said, on the corner of Rue des Belles-Feuilles and a blind alley of the same name. Tan façade, no balconies or ledges. Small, square windows, plus some shaped like portholes. The Lancia was parked at the end of the blind alley. To the right of the porch was a marble plaque with tarnished letters: "Furnished apartments."

It was already dark out. February? March? Drops of rain. Yvon and I had taken off our sweaters because the air was muggy.

A wide hallway with red velvet carpeting. On the left-hand side were glass doors. Winegrain was waiting in one of the doorways and motioned for us to come in.

It would have been hard to say whether it was a waiting room or a hotel dining room. Walls lined with plaid fabric. Round tables and dark wooden chairs. Bourdon, Leandri, and someone I didn't know were sprawled on the leather couch against the wall.

"Have a seat," said Winegrain.

We sat at one of the tables, on which were arranged cups, a teapot, a bottle of champagne, and glasses.

"Some tea?"

He filled two cups.

"Martine won't be long. She's upstairs, at Baby's . . ."

"He lives here?" Yvon asked in a blank voice.

"Yes. He rents a furnished room," said Winegrain.

The others were smoking in silence. Leandri had fallen asleep. The light came from a nearby lamp with a pink shade, and also, through two glass door panels, from a telephone booth fitted against the back wall.

"I'm delighted the two of you could be here," said Winegrain.

The others glanced at us with strange smiles.

"So: Martine is getting married to Baby," Winegrain resumed, in the sentential voice of a professor expounding a theorem. "Personally, I'm against it. How about you?"

"I don't know," said Yvon.

It was very hot in that room, and I was sweating. Yvon, too.

"But you're family. You can influence her . . . I think you have to talk to her . . ."

He poured himself a glass of champagne and downed it in one gulp. His cheeks were flushed. Something mean-spirited flashed in his eyes.

"I've known Baby for a long time. It would be a real mistake if she married Baby . . . especially . . ."

He squeezed Yvon's wrist.

"And don't go thinking I'm saying this out of jealousy . . ."

He turned toward the others as if calling for witnesses.

"You have no reason to be jealous of that guy," said Bourdon.

"I was just disappointed," sighed Winegrain. "Martine has disappointed me . . . I thought she had better taste . . ."

"Martine will do as she pleases," Yvon said sharply. "It's none of your business."

I wondered why we stayed seated in that room. Yvon must have had the same thought and stood up.

"Wait, hold on," said Winegrain. "I'm going to tell them to come down . . . They don't know you're here . . . It's a surprise . . ."

He lurched over to the telephone booth, pushed open the double doors with his shoulder, and slowly lifted the receiver. Yvon was on his feet.

He came out of the booth and patted Yvon on the shoulder.

"Baby will be right down . . . Your sister will be here soon."

We were seated again, eyes riveted on the elevator grate, to the left at the beginning of the hallway.

"It's like an oven in here," said Winegrain.

He went to open a window. The smell of rain and leaves invaded the room, and the wind slightly lifted the white cloth on our table. The elevator started down with a sharp, monotonous whine. The gate opened and out came da Silva. He entered the room and seemed surprised to see Yvon and me, but he didn't say hello. He was wearing a very sober navy blue suit.

"Where's Martine?" asked Winegrain.

"She's staying in bed," said da Silva in his strange, fluty voice. "And I have to go to work . . . I have to go meet a client at the Gare de Lyon, an American woman . . ."

"Will you be long?"

"No, I just have to drop her in Neuilly . . . The pain in the ass part is that I first have to go get the Daimler from the garage . . .

And the American sticks to me like glue. She says she can't fall asleep if I'm not there to hold her hand . . ."

Winegrain threw us furtive, curious glances, as if hoping to verify the effect these words were having on us. Was it the American woman's blue-white diamond that da Silva had given Martine as an engagement ring?

Da Silva disappeared into a storage closet next to the phone booth, and when he emerged he was wearing a chauffeur's navy blue cap with black visor. Oddly, the cap gave him an entirely different face from the one we were used to seeing. He had lost his childlike appearance, and instead had the pale, bloated skin of certain late-night bartenders, with squinty eyes and thin lips, the upper lip practically nonexistent. He looked both spineless and callous.

"So long, everybody . . . I won't be able to bring Martine home this evening. I'll leave that to you . . ."

Even his voice had changed. It had grown guttural.

"Are you going to Gaillon's tonight?" asked Winegrain.

"If the American drops off to sleep quick enough."

"If you do, play a hand for me."

Winegrain handed him a wad of cash. Da Silva counted it after moistening his finger with spit.

"Hope Lady Luck's with me tonight. Ciao!"

He spun on his heels with the self-conscious movement of a lounge dancer and left the room. After a moment, we heard the Lancia start up.

"And now it's time for the three of us to talk," said Winegrain, leaning toward us. "I'm depending on you to warn Martine . . . That guy's not Brazilian, and he's no millionaire . . ."

He let out a strangled little laugh.

"I met him when he worked in the bowling alley at Porte Maillot. Now he's a chauffeur. Next thing you know . . ."

Yvon had hung his head as if he didn't want to hear any of this.

"He calls himself da Silva, but his real name is Richard Mouliade . . . Mouliade . . . Mou-li-ade . . ."

That name, with its liquid sounds, made me feel queasy. It was like a whirlpool of silt, sucking in an entire body.

"Not only that, but he's got a record. He's really bad news for Martine . . ."

Again that strangled laugh. The floor was falling away under me. The room tilted and pitched. I was feeling very queasy. The wind swelled the tablecloth from underneath and I looked for something stable I could hold on to. My eyes latched on to a huge, unlit chandelier just above our heads, its prisms shining with drab brilliance.

"What can you do, the girl's in love," Winegrain muttered.

IX.

In autumn, we spent Monday afternoons doing what Mr. Jeanschmidt called "gardening": raking up the dead leaves from the lawns, the whole class in a row, working our way backward behind Pedro. And then we loaded the piles of leaves onto wheelbarrows that we went to dump in a vacant lot next to the changing hut.

One evening in May, during recess, Pedro had come upon me staring at the leaves on the large plane tree at the edge of the lawn.

"What are you thinking about, son?"

"The leaves we're going to have to rake up next fall, sir."

He knitted his brow.

"They're like students," Pedro answered gravely. "The old ones go, new ones come. The new ones turn old, and on and on . . . Just like the leaves."

I wondered then whether he kept any souvenirs, old report cards, old homework, from all those leaves that reappeared year after year.

Naturally, several "old ones" remained alive through school lore: Johnny, for instance, whose name was etched into one of the lockers in the changing hut, with its odor of wet wood, next to which we emptied our wheelbarrows in the fall . . . Pedro had told us the story of Johnny so many times that I felt as if I knew him as well as my actual classmates.

Whenever I think of Johnny, I picture him in his grandmother's apartment on Avenue du Général-Balfourier. Someone must have been looking after the place in her absence, as there was no dust on the furniture and the parquet floors shone so brightly that Johnny, feeling intimidated, walked on eggshells.

In late afternoon, the sun drew a large, sand-colored rectangle in the middle of the carpet. The light coated the walls and bookshelves in gauze, like the slipcovers people drape over furniture in unused apartments. Sitting on the sofa, Johnny stretched out his leg, and the shoe on his right foot reached the center of the bright spot on the carpet. Not moving, he pondered the sunlight glancing off the black leather, and soon it felt as if the shoe were no longer connected to his body. A shoe abandoned for all eternity inside a rectangle of light. Gradually darkness fell. They had shut off the electricity, and as twilight slowly invaded the apartment he felt more and more anxious. Why had he stayed in Paris all alone? What made him do it? No doubt the numbness and paralysis of nightmares, when one is trying to flee danger or hop a train . . .

And yet, the weather in Paris was beautiful that year, and Johnny had turned twenty-two. His real name was Kurt, but for years they had called him Johnny because of his likeness to Johnny Weissmuller, the swimmer and movie star he admired.

Johnny was particularly good at skiing, the fine points of which he had learned from instructors in St. Anton, when he and his grandmother still lived in Austria. He wanted to become a professional skier.

He even thought he was following in Weissmuller's footsteps the day he was offered a walk-on part in a mountaineering film. Sometime after it was shot, he and his grandmother had left Austria because of the Anschluss. In France, he was enrolled in the Valvert School, and had remained there until the war broke out.

Now, every evening at around eight-thirty, he left his grandmother's empty apartment and took the metro to Passy. The elevated station was like the tiny depot of a winter resort or the last stop of a funicular. Descending the stairs, he reached the buildings lower down, near the Square de l'Alboni, in that tiered section of Passy reminiscent of Monte Carlo.

On the top floor of one of those buildings lived a woman fifteen years his senior, a certain Arlette d'Alwyn, whom he had met in April in a café on Avenue Delessert. She had told him she was married to a fighter pilot, from whom she hadn't had word since the start of the war. She thought he might be in Syria or London. Prominently displayed at the edge of the nightstand was a garnet leather frame containing the photo of a handsome, dark-haired man: pencil mustache, aviator's uniform. But the photo looked like a movie still. And why was only her name, Arlette d'Alwyn, engraved on the copper plaque on the door of the apartment?

She gave him a key to her place, and in the evening, when

he entered the living room, she was stretched out on the divan, nude beneath her dressing gown. She was playing a record. She was blonde, with green eyes and very soft skin, and even though she was fifteen years older, she looked as young as Johnny, with something dreamy and vaporous about her. But she had a temper.

She arranged to see him at 9 p.m. She wasn't free during the day, and he had to leave her apartment very early in the morning. He was curious about how she spent her time, but she eluded his questions. One evening, he had arrived shortly before her and rifled haphazardly through a chest of drawers, where he found a receipt from the pawnshop on Rue Pierre-Charron. That was how he learned she had hocked a ring, a pin, and some earrings, and for the first time he caught a slight whiff of ruin in that apartment, a bit like at his grandmother's. Was it the smell of opiates that impregnated the furniture, the bed, the record player, the empty shelves, and the photo of the supposed fighter pilot framed in garnet-colored leather?

His situation was difficult, too. He had not left Paris in two years, since the month of May 1940, when he had brought his grandmother to Saint-Nazaire. She had taken the last boat for America, and tried to persuade him to go with her. Their visas were in order. He had said he preferred to stay in France, that he was in no danger. Before departure time, the two of them had sat on a bench in the little square near the docks.

In Paris, he had tried to reconnect with former classmates from the Valvert School. No luck. Then he had haunted the various film studios, looking for work as an extra, but he needed a guild card and they weren't issuing any to Jews, much less to foreign Jews like him. He had gone to the Racing Club to see whether they needed a gymnastics trainer. Waste of time. He thought of spending the winter in a ski resort, where he might secure a job as an instructor. But since they were in the Unoccupied Zone, how could he get there?

By chance he came across a want ad: they were looking for people to model Morreton hats. They hired him. He posed in a studio on Boulevard Delessert, and it was after work one day that he had met Arlette d'Alwyn. They photographed him head-on, in profile, in three-quarter view, each time wearing a Morreton hat of a different style or color. That line of work required what the photographer called a "good mug," as a hat accentuates the face's defects. You need a straight nose, a well-formed chin, and nicely arched brows—all qualities he possessed. It had lasted a month and then they'd let him go.

After that, he had sold off some furniture from the apartment on Avenue du Général-Balfourier, where he'd lived with his grandmother. He went through moments of depression and anxiety. Nothing good could happen in this city. He felt trapped. All things considered, he should have gone to America.

At first, to keep his spirits up, he resumed his habit of a rigorous exercise routine. Every morning, he went to the Deligny public pool, or to the Bérétrot pool in Joinville-le-Pont. He swam the crawl and the breaststroke for an hour. But soon he felt so isolated among those indifferent men and women, with their sun-bathing and paddleboating, that he stopped going to Deligny or Joinville altogether.

He rested indoors on Avenue du Général-Balfourier, and at eight o'clock he would go out to see Arlette d'Alwyn.

Why, on certain evenings, did he put off his departure? He would gladly have remained alone in the empty apartment with its closed shutters. Back when, his grandmother used to scold him gently for being distracted and uncommunicative, for lacking in "social skills" and not taking care of himself, such as always going out in the rain or snow without a coat: "in shirtsleeves," as she put it. But by now, it was too late to fix this. One day, he didn't feel up to leaving Avenue du Général-Balfourier. The next evening, he had shown up at Arlette d'Alwyn's tousled and unkempt, and she said she'd been worried about him and that such a handsome, distinguished young man oughtn't let himself go like that.

The air was so warm and the night so clear that they left the windows open. They set out the velvet cushions from the divan in the middle of the small balcony and lay there until very late. On the top floor of a neighboring building, on a balcony like theirs, stood several people whose laughter they could hear.

Johnny was still nurturing his idea about winter sports. Arlette was not very familiar with the mountains. She had been to Sestrières once and remembered it fondly. Why not go there together? As for Johnny, he was thinking about Switzerland.

Another time, the evening was warm and he decided not to

get off at the Passy stop, as he usually did, but at Trocadéro. He would walk to Arlette's via the gardens and the Quai de Passy.

He reached the top of the metro stairs and saw a cordon of police standing guard on the sidewalk. They asked to see his papers. He didn't have any. They shoved him into a police van a bit farther on, which already contained a dozen other shadowy figures.

It was one of the roundups that, in the past few months, had routinely preceded convoys to the East.

X.

Every two weeks, at evening study hall, one of our teachers would announce our "categories." Pedro had decided on these during a teachers' meeting. Category A meant very good work, and B, passable work. Category C was reserved for those who had committed disciplinary infractions and lost their exit privileges.

On Saturday mornings, we assembled behind the Castle, in a fallow field with a lone Lebanese cedar. Pedro called the roll of C's and, one by one, the unfortunates went to stand in a row at the edge of the field. The C's would spend Saturday and Sunday at the school doing yard work and marching in quickstep along the paths.

Some of the A's and B's waited for their parents to come, but most of us climbed into the two Chausson buses that had idled in front of the Castle since nine-thirty. When everyone was seated, the two buses jerked into motion and, one following the other, rolled slowly down the drive. After the main gate, they turned onto the highway. Then all the students, older and younger, struck up campfire songs or barracks ditties in chorus.

My classmate Christian Portier and I never sang those songs, and perhaps that was why we got along so well. We always sat next to each other on the bus. For several months, on our Saturdays and Sundays out, we were inseparable.

Christian's mother came to collect us at the bus stop at Porte de Saint-Cloud, and the image of Mme Portier—Claude Portier—waiting for us at the wheel of her Renault convertible, cigarette dangling from her lips, has remained indelibly etched in my memory.

She smoked Royales. With graceful movements, she pulled the red cigarette pack from her handbag. The click of her bag as it snapped shut, the breath of perfume it exhaled. The smell of her Royales—that bitter, slightly sickening odor of French blond tobacco . . . She was on the small side, with light brown hair and gray eyes, and her cheekbones, stubborn forehead, and short nose gave her face a catlike quality. She looked just like the movie actress Yvette Lebon. Moreover, early in our friendship, Christian had me convinced that he was the son of Yvette Lebon, and when I first met his mother he gestured toward her ceremoniously and said:

"Allow me to introduce Yvette Lebon."

It must have been their private joke, or a way for Christian to show her off. She had probably mentioned the resemblance years before, when Christian was too young to know who Yvette Lebon was. Perhaps she had even taught him the phrase, "Allow me to introduce Yvette Lebon," and he repeated his lesson, uncomprehending, to the delight of Mme Portier's friends. Yes, I could easily imagine Christian, with his big head and prematurely deep voice, as his mother's pageboy.

Those Saturdays, when the bus brought us from the Valvert School to Paris, we arrived at Porte de Saint-Cloud at around noon, and Mme Portier took us to lunch in a restaurant near the bus stop. A wide balcony with a copper railing, and a dining room below. We sat at a table on the balcony, Mme Portier and her son next to each other, me facing them.

Mme Portier ate like a bird: she ordered a hard-boiled egg, grapefruit . . . Christian looked at her sternly and said:

"Claude, you really should eat something."

He called her by her first name, and at first I had been surprised to hear this fifteen-year-old gently bossing his mother around.

"Claude, that's your fifth cigarette . . . Give me the pack, right now."

He plucked the cigarette from her mouth, stubbed it out, and confiscated her pack of Royales. Mme Portier bowed her head submissively and smiled.

"Claude, I think you've lost more weight. You're not being sensible."

His mother looked straight back at him, and soon, like two children having a staring contest, they burst out laughing. They were playing it up for my benefit.

Every other Saturday, Mme Portier didn't come to pick us up at Porte de Saint-Cloud; she would send a telegram to Valvert the evening before to let us know. She was sleeping in after having stayed up all night playing poker. On those Saturdays, we got into the habit of waking her at three in the afternoon with breakfast in bed.

There was never any mention of a "Mr. Portier," and I wondered whether Christian had a father. Finally, one Sunday evening when we were back in school, he opened up to me, speaking in a low voice so as not to wake our bunkmates. We leaned against the windowsill, and the great lawn below shone pale green in the moonlight. No, his mother had never been married and had kept her maiden name, Portier. He, Christian, was a love child. His father? A Greek, whom Claude had known in Paris during the Occupation. He now lived in Brazil, and Christian had seen him only two or three times in his life.

I wanted to know more about this mysterious Greek, but I didn't dare ask Mme Portier.

In the afternoon, Claude took Christian shopping, and I went with them. One Saturday, we went to pick up Mme Portier's present for her son's fifteenth birthday, a flannel suit. It was November or December and already growing dark. Mme Portier guided us through a run-down apartment on Rue du Colisée, as if she knew the place well. A huge space, desk lamps fastened to long tables, fabric samples, a fireplace, a mirrored armoire, a leather sofa. The tailor, a man of about sixty with chubby cheeks and muttonchops, greeted us and kissed Mme Portier's hand, but with a certain familiarity.

Christian was excited to try on his first suit. The tailor lit a neon tube at the top of one of the mirrors on the armoire, then opened the two side doors. And my friend, reflected from every angle, stood up straight in his "dark flannel" and blinked, dazzled by the bright neon glare.

"What's your verdict, young man?"

The tailor spun him around, pushing his shoulder, and examined the trouser pleats.

"And you, my dear, are you pleased with your son's first suit?"

"Very pleased," said Mme Portier. "As long as there's no vest."

"Someday you'll have to explain to me your aversion to vests."

"Nothing to explain . . . I've always found men who sported vests or chinstrap beards ridiculous."

She grabbed me by the wrist.

"Take my advice: if you want women like me to like you, *never* wear a vest . . . or grow a chinstrap beard."

"Don't listen to my mother," said Christian. "She sometimes gets these absurd notions . . ."

The tailor had taken a step back and his gaze caressed Christian's suit.

"The young man has almost exactly the same measurements as his father. You know, I found an old index card on your father . . ."

Mme Portier knitted her brow slightly.

"What a memory you have, dear Elston!"

Christian came forward in his suit.

"Perhaps you could give me the card. To remember him by."

But he had said it without conviction. He walked toward the

fitting room at the other end of the space, gingerly, like a tight-rope walker on his wire. Perhaps he was afraid of getting a splinter in his foot.

Mme Portier, sitting on the sofa, lit a cigarette.

"I remember that you came by with his father very late one evening to pick up a suit. And they were bombing . . . But we didn't go down to the cellar."

"That's all ancient history," Mme Portier said, letting her cigarette ash fall on the floor.

"I went looking through all those old documents to see how long we've known each other . . ."

Mme Portier shrugged. Christian had come up to us.

"What were you talking about?" he said.

"About the past," said Mme Portier. "Do you like your suit?"

"Thank you, Claude."

He bent over and kissed his mother's forehead.

"You should wear it this evening," said Mme Portier.

"As you wish, Claude."

And there, in front of us, he changed clothes again, removing his corduroy pants and sweater and slipping on the "dark flannel."

Mme Portier took her son's arm and led him out of the room. The tailor and I walked behind them.

"Good-bye, my dear. And thank you again for thinking of me for this suit."

His gaze lingered on the "dark flannel" that my friend was

wearing, and that shone with a funereal glow in the yellow light of the stairway.

Mme Portier held out her hand.

"Elston . . . Do you think I've aged?"

"Aged? Not in the slightest . . ."

Christian bowed his head, embarrassed.

"Are you sure? Now that he's old enough to wear a suit, I won't be able to cheat anymore . . ."

"First of all, no one would ever think that this strapping young fellow is your son. You haven't aged a day, my dear . . ."

He had enunciated those last words, hammering out each syllable. The hall light went off. Elston pressed the switch again. He watched after us, leaning on the railing, as we walked down the stairs.

■

Now that my friend owned the "dark flannel," I felt a bit ashamed of my old wool blazer with its gold buttons and the high-water pants that made me look even younger than my fifteen years. Christian's mother gave me a silk tie. I wore it for all of our outings and it restored a bit of my self-confidence.

On summer evenings, she treated us to dinner on the banks of the Seine. Was it in Rueil? Chatou? Bougival? I've tried several times to find that inn. Without success. The outskirts of Paris have changed so much . . . Below was a large wooden platform lined with cabins, two diving boards, a slide. A line of paddleboats was moored to the pontoon. We could hear the dull, rhythmic drone of cascades, perhaps the Marly waterwheels. A sparsely graveled terrace. The houseboats floated among the willows on the banks, and my eyes followed the green light on the prow of one of them. When we were finished dining on the terrace, a heavyset fellow with gray hair came to sit at our table, the owner of the inn, a certain Jendron. He, too, was wearing a blazer, but much more elegant than mine, and a sailor sweater. He looked about a decade older than Mme Portier. He always offered Christian and me American cigarettes, and he called Mme Portier "Claudie."

The snatches of their conversation blended with the tepid air of those evenings, the slap of the paddleboats against the pontoon dock, the smell of the Seine . . . Jendron had managed a garage before the war, which had also employed a certain Pagnon, whose name cropped up often in their conversation: a friend of Mme Portier's, since she called him "Eddy." Whatever could have happened to that Eddy Pagnon, for them to mention him in such whispers? It all predated Christian's birth. Had Jendron known the Greek, Christian's father? My friend wasn't listening, but instead slipped off in the clear night to the pontoon dock and took a paddleboat. I preferred to stay at the table with Jendron and Claudie. I wanted to understand.

At around midnight, we crossed the large platform, moonlight casting the shadows of the slide and the diving boards onto the wooden planks. At that instant, it was as if we were in Cap d'Antibes. We went looking for Christian, who was playing ping-pong with the bartender.

Jendron walked us to our car. He patted Christian on the back of the neck.

"So, you working hard?"

And my friend, despite his "dark flannel," looked like a small boy next to that corpulent man.

"What do you want to do with yourself?"

Christian, feeling shy, didn't answer.

"Can I give you a piece of advice? Become a lawyer."

He turned to me.

"Don't you think that's a good thing, being a lawyer?"

He shoved into each of our jacket pockets two packs of American cigarettes.

"What do you think, Claudie? Like to have a lawyer for a son?"

"Sure, why not?"

We climbed into the convertible. Christian, although he wasn't old enough to have a license, sat at the wheel. Mme Portier sat next to him, and I on the back seat.

"You shouldn't let him drive, Claudie . . ."

"I know."

She nodded, in a sign of helplessness. Christian peeled off. He got onto the westbound highway. The night was warm and silent, the road empty. He turned on the radio. I leaned out from the car and the air whipped my face. I felt dizzy and happy.

He handed Claudie the wheel just before the Saint-Cloud tunnel.

■

Mme Portier lived in a building on the corner of Avenue Paul-Doumer and Rue de La Tour, with a glass entrance door. I don't have a very clear memory of her apartment, except for the sitting room, half-living room, half-dining room, which was divided by a cast-iron grate; and the bedroom, with its gray satin wall covering, where we brought her breakfast on the afternoons after poker.

The first Saturday afternoon they brought me to their home, we drank orangeade in the living room. Christian seemed impatient, as if he had prepared a surprise or prank and was waiting for an opportune moment to spring it.

Mme Portier smiled. I looked for something to say.

"You have a very lovely apartment."

"Very lovely," said Christian. Then he turned to his mother. "Shall we tell him, Claude?"

"Yes, tell him."

"It's like this, old man," Christian said, moving his face close to mine. "I don't live in my mother's apartment . . ."

She had lit a cigarette. The insipid odor of the Royale mixed with her perfume.

"Last year, Claude and I decided, by mutual agreement . . ."

He paused for a moment. Mme Portier walked to the other end of the room and picked up the telephone.

"We decided not to get in each other's way . . . That's why Claude rented me a room, here in the building, on the ground floor."

I was listening to Christian, but I would also have liked to know what she was saying on the phone.

"Don't you think that's a good solution?" asked Christian. "This way, we each have our own lives . . ."

Who could she have been speaking to in such a low voice, almost a whisper? She hung up.

"Claude, we'll be leaving," said Christian. "I'm going to show him my place. Shall we get together this evening?"

"I might not be free," said Mme Portier. "Call me around six."

"Claude got them to install a telephone in my room," Christian told me, looking delighted.

Pinned to his door was a calling card with the name Christian Portier. The room, about the size of a ship's cabin, looked out on Avenue Paul-Doumer through a sash window. Christian's bed was covered with a plaid blanket. An armchair in the same fabric against the tan wall. A long shelf supported model airplanes and a globe of the world. A photo of Yvette Lebon on the opposite wall. Or was it Mme Portier? Christian caught me looking.

"You're wondering which one it is, right? Claude or Yvette?"

He folded his arms, like a schoolteacher who has just asked his student a trick question.

"It's Claude, old man."

He was proud to show me the ivory-colored radio integrated

into the nightstand. Then the narrow bathroom, with its navy blue tiling and hip bath.

"You mind if we listen to the radio?" he asked.

He turned the dial. An announcer said, "For those who love jazz." A trumpet played a slow, serene melody, like the trajectory of a seabird hovering above a deserted beach at dusk.

"Hear that? That's Sonny Berman . . ."

We were both sitting on the edge of his bed. Christian had taken a bottle of whiskey from the closet and half-filled his toothbrush glass. We took turns drinking while listening to the music, and the shadows of passersby, projected against the wall by a streetlamp in the avenue, brushed over us.

■

On those Saturday evenings we were often alone, just the two of us, and we dined like adults in an empty restaurant on Square de l'Alboni, thanks to the fifty francs in pocket money that Mme Portier gave her son.

"I'm writing all this down in the accounts book," he'd told me, "and I'll reimburse Claude when I turn twenty-one."

Then we went by metro to the ten o'clock showing at a cinema in Auteuil. Christian had told me that the manager of this movie house was a friend of his mother's. My schoolmate went up to the window and the cashier immediately handed him two complimentary tickets.

We walked back home via Rue Chardon-Lagache and Rue

La Fontaine. I was wearing my duffel coat and Christian a camel-hair coat, over his dark flannel. The outfit made him look ten years older, but apparently that still wasn't enough: he had bought tortoiseshell eyeglass frames that he put on for our outings with his mother. If he could have, he'd have grown a mustache and dyed his hair gray.

In the building's cream-green foyer, he proposed under his breath:

"What say we go drop in on Claude . . . ?"

Exiting the elevator, he tiptoed up to the apartment, and we remained standing, motionless in front of the door. The timer in the hall light ran out and neither of us thought to turn it back on. Muffled shouts or bursts of laughter. How many guests were there? Now and then I recognized Mme Portier's voice, but different from the one she used during the day, throatier—as was her laugh, more strident and staccato than normal.

After a moment, he took my arm and guided me through the darkness.

Once again, we found ourselves in the foyer, whose walls gleamed in the garish light of the sconces.

"I'll walk you to the metro . . ."

It was right nearby, at Place du Trocadéro. Often, to spend a few more moments together, we circled Trocadéro and followed Avenue Kléber to the next station, Boissière.

"Claude is still throwing her little shindig," Christian said. "Or else playing poker."

He affected an amused tone.

"She's going to have one heck of a hangover tomorrow . . ."

As we parted company, I noticed his tense features and sad eyes. The prospect of going home alone to Avenue Paul-Doumer, to his independent room, must not have seemed very appealing. And Claude, who was "throwing her little shindig" . . . No doubt he would have liked to confide in me just then, but he pulled back. Before I went down the metro steps, he waved and pressed his fingers against his temple in a vague military salute.

Much later, I understood that—unlike those mature men who labor to suck in their guts and step lively to look younger— behind the tortoiseshell glasses, the dark flannel suit and camel-hair coat, there was only a frightened child.

■

That kind of man, of a certain age but still slim, or at least trying to appear so by minding his posture—I had seen several of them with Mme Portier. She had come to visit us at school a few times in the company of one or another of them, never the same one. She always chose the moment when we were on the great lawn for afternoon recess, before evening study hall.

She introduced us to a "Mr. Weiler" with silver hair and heavy eyelids. He asked Christian a few amiable questions about his studies. He gave off a scent of chypre and kept crumpling a pair of gloves with his slender fingers. After that visit, Christian told me that this Weiler was a very rich diamond merchant whom his mother had met not long before. Another one, a blond with a mustache and athletic bearing, the marquis de Something-or-other, spoke in a booming voice and used slang. While Mme Portier brought Weiler in her car, whenever she came to school with "the Marquis," it was in the latter's Buick.

The profile of a third man, with a sly face and a black overcoat . . . That one, Christian and I nicknamed "the Weasel." To which of the three — or was it a fourth — had Christian, one afternoon when we were alone in his mother's apartment, answered on the telephone with the perfect manner of a private secretary: Miss Portier is out but I'll tell her you called . . . Miss Portier will surely not be home before seven this evening . . . Very well, I'll be sure to let Miss Portier know . . ."

Still today, I wonder why she made those visits to Valvert. Was she perhaps trying to reassure all those men by showing them her big son, boarder in a renowned school just outside Paris? And what of Christian's "independent" room? I suppose it came in handy when Miss Portier welcomed her friends to her apartment on Saturday nights.

■

One Saturday evening, in fact, I rang at her door. Christian had been grounded because he got a zero in math, and he had given me a letter for his mother, along with a small tin valise full of laundry.

She opened the door. She was barefoot and wrapped in a white terrycloth robe. She seemed embarrassed to see me.

"Oh, hello . . . This is a surprise . . ."

She stood there, in the doorway, as if to keep me from entering.

"Who is it, Claude?" came a man's voice from the living room.

"No one . . . A friend of my son's . . ."

And after a moment's hesitation:

"Please, come in."

He was sitting on one of the leather ottomans, torso arched forward, like a jockey facing a hurdle. He looked up and smiled at me. It was not Weiler, or the Marquis, or the Weasel, but a dark-haired man of around fifty with a slightly ruddy complexion and blue eyes.

Mme Portier unsealed Christian's letter. I held onto the small valise.

"Have a seat," he said.

She read the letter, then gave out a brief laugh.

"My son recommends that I not stay up too late, smoke less, and quit playing poker . . ."

"Your son's right."

He turned to me.

"Would you care for some tea?"

He pointed to a tray on the coffee table, with two cups and a teapot.

"No, thank you."

"So you're a friend of her son's?"

"Yes."

"And what's he doing at the moment?"

"He's at school . . . He's been grounded . . ."

Mme Portier had shoved the letter into a pocket of her bathrobe. She went to sit on the edge of the couch and crossed her legs. A flap of her robe slid open, revealing her thighs. Her olive skin, between the white terrycloth of the robe and the red velvet of the couch, held my gaze.

"Poor Christian," she said, "he must be so bored there all alone . . . What about you, Ludo — did they ever ground you when you were little?"

Ludo shrugged.

"I never went to school . . . My mother found some guy to teach me and my brother to read . . . And also a gym instructor."

I could hardly tear my eyes away from Mme Portier's long, olive thighs.

"What if we paid your son a visit?" he said. "It might buck up his spirits."

Had she already brought him to the school, like Weiler, the Marquis, and the Weasel?

"It's too late now," said Mme Portier. "And it's cold out . . ."

I thought of Christian. An entire afternoon of "gardening" would be followed by dinner time. He would eat in the back of the empty dining hall, with another twenty or so classmates who had been kept in like him. They would not be allowed to speak to one another. After that would come the silent walk, in single file, to the dormitory.

Ludo stood up and held out a cigarette case.

"Smoke?"

"No, thank you."

"Tell Christian I'll come see him on Tuesday," Mme Portier said to me.

"I'll come with you, Claude."

It was a veritable ritual. Was Christian, with his natural meticulousness, drawing up a list of all the men his mother had brought to visit him since he'd been a boarder at Valvert?

She caught me looking and quickly pulled the robe back over her knees.

"It won't be much fun for you, spending the weekend without Christian," she said.

"I guess not."

"You can stay with us if you like," said Ludo.

He was resting his elbow on the marble mantelpiece. I was struck by the grace of his posture. It came from the elegant cut of his suit, but also from a natural nonchalance in crossing his arms and legs and holding himself at a slight angle.

"I don't know, we could . . . play bridge, the four of us, with my brother . . ."

"Don't be silly, Ludo. The young man doesn't play bridge."

"A pity . . ."

She saw me to the door, and as I was taking my leave, her face was so close to mine, and her perfume so alluring, that I felt like kissing her. Why wasn't I allowed to kiss her?

"My friend is very nice, you know . . . Christian is very fond of him. Ludo is going to teach him how to pilot a plane. You can come too, if you like . . . He was a flying ace during the war . . ."

She smiled at me. In the living room, Ludo had put a record on the phonograph.

"So long . . . And don't forget to tell Christian I'll come see him on Tuesday."

Walking down the stairs, I realized I was still holding the small tin valise containing my friend's dirty laundry.

Inadvertently, or to have an excuse to go back to Mme Portier's apartment?

■

Night had fallen. Still carrying the valise, I went into a self-service restaurant on the avenue, across from their building. I was the only customer. I selected a yogurt and a slice of pie at the counter and sat down at one of the circular tables near the window.

A half-hour later, I saw Ludo leave the building. Now it was my turn to go back up to the apartment, on the pretext of giving Mme Portier the valise. And once upstairs . . . But when I reached the sidewalk, I hesitated; then, like an automaton, I started following Ludo.

He was walking about twenty yards ahead of me. He opened the door of a large brown car parked on the corner of Rue Scheffer and took out a coat, which he didn't put on but rather draped over his shoulders. He walked off down Rue Scheffer.

As I went by, I noticed, propped against the car window, a plaque bearing the words "Severely Disabled Veteran," precariously balanced between two packets of paper handkerchiefs and a stack of Michelin roadmaps. That neglected plaque reminded me of his nonchalant grace when he rested his elbow on the mantel.

Now he pushed on toward Boulevard Delessert, draped in that navy blue overcoat as if it were a cape, and glanced at those mysterious stairways, on either side of the boulevard, that flank the buildings. He had a slight limp. Severely disabled veteran. Flying ace, as Mme Portier had said. I was nothing compared to this man. Why was I following him? I would have liked to talk to him about Claude, ask him questions, for we had one thing in common: we both knew that peppery perfume that blended with the smell of Royales and those olive thighs beneath the terrycloth robe.

He halted at the bottom of the avenue, where the Trocadéro gardens began. I did, too. I set down the valise on the gravel. No, I would never have the nerve to approach him. He was smoking. With a flick of his finger, he launched the butt into the air, raising his chin as if to follow the trajectory of a shooting star.

Both of us, that winter night, had arrived at the flank of a hill, from where we could see the lights of Paris, the Seine, the horses on the Pont d'Iéna. A tour boat passed by, and its searchlights ran over the façades lining the quays and across the gardens.

■

After I left the Valvert School, I lost touch with Christian and Mme Portier.

Twenty years later, in Nice, I was looking for a cheap hotel or boardinghouse for an old friend of my father's who wanted to spend the winter there. It was November and already dark out. At the end of Rue Shakespeare, after the cream-colored buildings with names of flowers above the door, there was a sign on a fence: "Villa Sainte-Anne. Furnished studios. Kitchen with fridge. Bath. Garden. Sunny. Oil heat."

A sparsely graveled driveway led to a half-open gate. The garden was dimly lit by the yellow light from the porch, leaving a patch of lawn in semidarkness: the sound of rabbit hutches or birdcages, possibly the rustle of wings.

I climbed the porch steps. Behind the French doors, a living room with papered walls. Rustic furniture. A table with a lace tablecloth. And the light was so yellow, so faded, that it looked as if the current had been lowered. A woman was sitting at the table, arms folded, watching television.

I knocked on the glass but she didn't hear. I pushed open the doors. She turned around.

Mme Portier.

She got up and came toward me, turning off the TV on the way.

"Good evening . . ."

"Good evening . . . Do you still have a studio for rent?"

"Yes, indeed . . ."

I had recognized her immediately. Her face was more or less

unchanged, but puffier, her hair much shorter. Her mouth was slightly pinched in a bitter expression. Her eyes still had that very diluted gray or blue sparkle that had so moved me.

"Will you be staying long?"

"Yes, about two months."

"In that case, I'll show you the unit with a bathroom and kitchen . . ."

We circled around the house and she preceded me up a narrow staircase, its steps covered in linoleum. A hallway lit by a bare bulb on the wall. A door.

"Go on in."

She turned on the light. The wooden ceiling fixture looked like a ship's tiller into which they'd stuck light bulbs with parchment lampshades. The same linoleum as in the stairwell. Wallpaper with dark red patterns. A brass bed.

"Over here's the kitchenette."

In a closet, they had installed an ancient-model stove and a small, wheezing refrigerator.

"Would you like to see the bathroom?"

We again filed down the hallway. She opened a door. A white enamel clawfoot tub.

"Toilet's across the hall."

"Can I see the room again?" I asked.

"Of course."

The curtains were drawn. They, too, had dark red patterns — leaf shapes — just like the wallpaper. It smelled musty.

"Is the window facing the street?" I asked.

"No, the garden."

With a casual movement, she opened the drapes.

"And may I ask how much?"

"Twelve hundred a month."

Suddenly she looked much older, perhaps because she hadn't put on any makeup.

I went up to her.

"You wouldn't be Mme Portier, by any chance?"

Her eyes widened, as if I were threatening her with a gun.

"Why? Do you know me?"

"Yes. A long time ago . . . I was a friend of Christian's."

"Ah, a friend of Christian's . . . You were a friend of Christian's . . ."

She repeated the phrase with a kind of relief.

"We were at the Valvert School together . . . when you lived on Avenue Paul-Doumer . . ."

"Avenue Paul-Doumer . . ."

She focused her gaze on me.

"I don't recognize you . . . What was your name again?"

"Patrick."

"Patrick . . . Yes, of course . . . Yes, I remember."

She gave me a smile and sat on the edge of the bed.

"You know, I no longer go by Portier. Life is complicated . . ."

And full of unexpected twists. I never would have imagined that one evening, in Nice, I would find myself in a hotel room with Mme Portier.

"I'm married now . . . to a guy who's twenty years older than me . . ."

She smoothed the fringes on the bedspread.

"I've had my share of ups and downs . . ."

"And what about Christian?" I asked.

"He lives in Canada. I haven't heard from him in ages. I think he's cut me off . . ."

"How come?"

She shrugged.

"He must hold something against me . . . Basically, I never should have had kids. The old guy I'm married to doesn't even know I had a son."

"So why did you get married?"

It was an indiscreet question, but there, in that room, she would tell me anything.

"Truth be told, I was broke."

Her blue-gray eyes brightened when she smiled.

"My husband is an old pain in the ass who might live to be a hundred . . . I act as his housekeeper. Isn't that a kick? Can you picture me doing that?"

I didn't know what to answer.

"So, you want the room?"

"It wouldn't be for me, but for a friend."

"So what do you do for a living?"

She had caught me off-guard.

"Oh . . . nothing much . . . I write detective novels."

"I'm not surprised you've become a writer. You were always a bit of a dreamer, weren't you?"

She stood up.

"You'll have to write a novel about me. My life's a story with a tragic ending."

She let out a loud laugh, the same laugh I'd liked so much back on Avenue Paul-Doumer.

"You get a load of the room? Pretty ugly, huh? Everything about this place is gloomy . . . My husband has no taste. And a lousy temper to boot. Like all old men."

She pulled me out of the room and took my arm to go downstairs.

"You want to see my hideout? It's the only place where he can't come pester me."

At the edge of the garden stood a tiny square lodge that a guard or concierge might have lived in. She opened the door.

"The old fart doesn't have the key . . . Sometimes I lock myself in here."

A chandelier. An Empire bed. Pieces of furniture stacked atop each other. Mirrors. Lamps. Suitcases. An Egyptian Revival writing desk. And photos tacked to the walls.

"This is what I managed to save from the wreckage . . . These were all at Avenue Paul-Doumer."

One of the photos was of her as a very young blonde, with bangs and bright eyes, wearing a satin jumpsuit with see-through lace motifs. She was resting her head on the arm of a settee and her outstretched right leg rested on the other arm. Her left leg was bent. She had on black high-heeled pumps.

"I was eighteen there. The manager of the Société des Bains de Mer in Monaco was wild about me . . . He introduced me to Prince Pierre . . ."

A smaller photo: her on horseback, next to another rider.

"That was with Pagnon, a friend from Asnières. He worked for the Germans . . . He got Christian's father and me released after we were arrested . . ."

She picked up a pillow from the floor and pulled the red velvet bedspread over the rumpled sheets.

"The Germans beat the crap out of us . . . I wonder what Christian's father could have been up to . . . They nearly knocked my teeth out."

She lifted a painting that had been laid askew on the nightstand.

"Can you help me with this? I want to put it back there . . ."

I leaned the painting against the wall.

"It's a real junk room here. I've got so many souvenirs. Maybe you'd be interested for your detective stories . . ."

"I'm very interested," I said.

"Well, then, you'll have to come back some afternoon to poke around . . ."

We crossed the garden. She had slipped on an old red anorak that barely reached her waist, its color vivid against the black of her trousers. She motioned toward the cages in the shadows.

"I've got about twenty birds I'm raising—it helps pass the time . . ."

"Isn't that hard work?"

"Oh, no. I've done much harder things than that."

Again she took my arm as we walked down the gravel drive. She had the same supple, gliding step as in the days of Valvert.

"I was even a circus rider when I was young."

"A circus rider?"

"If your friend rents the studio, we can see each other more often . . ."

"I'd like that."

We had reached the gate. She leaned her face closer to mine.

"Do you think I've aged a lot?"

"No."

And it was true that, in the muted light of the street, her face regained its smoothness. In any case, her supple gait and her laugh hadn't changed a bit.

"I've got to go make my husband his soup. He hasn't said a word to me all week. He's giving me the cold shoulder . . . Anyway, it's impossible having a conversation—he's deaf as a post. He's in bed by nine . . ."

"Would you like to have dinner some evening?"

She nodded solemnly.

"Yes, but in that case I'll have to give you an address and phone number where you can leave a message. The old man is always on my back, you understand? He even opens my mail."

She felt around the pocket of her anorak and handed me a calling card.

"This is my hairdresser . . . Christian always wrote me at this address."

"Too bad the three of us can't get together," I said.

She rested a hand on my shoulder.

"You really are quite the dreamer . . ."

Once on the sidewalk, I looked back. She was standing at the fence, forehead pressed against the bars. She smiled.

"Don't forget. Rue Pastorelli . . . Condé Coiffure . . ."

XI.

It was nine in the evening and I was walking past a waiting room in the Gare du Nord.

A face. Forehead resting on that aquariumlike window, eyes anxious and weary. That was you, Charell.

I rapped on the glass. He recognized me as well. After twenty years, we had hardly changed, or at least Charell hadn't. He stood up and stared at me, blinking, as if I'd suddenly stepped out of a dream. His distinguished blond mien stood out among the rare individuals who had washed up there: a sleeping vagrant, his head on the shoulder of an old woman in a raincoat and too much makeup; a gaunt-faced Arab whose brand-new glen plaid suit tapered at the ankles, revealing sneakers without laces. Over that waiting room, with its brown wood paneling and muted light, floated a smell of urine.

"Funny running into you here, old man," said Charell.

He was making a visible effort to appear relaxed, like someone who has just been caught in dubious surroundings or circumstances and tries to ward off suspicion.

"No reason we have to stay here . . ."

He took my arm and guided me firmly through the train station, glancing left and right with that same worried look he'd had moments before, behind the glass. What was he afraid of? That I might see him meet someone?

Taking the exit on the building's left flank, we emerged into a wide blind alley. We could hear shouts and whispers from groups of shadows, motionless in the dark. We nearly tripped over bodies sitting on the sidewalk, surrounded by suitcases and overnight bags. Against the alley's open gates stood some very young girls in leather jackets; one of them wore a black headband that canceled her forehead and masked one eye. And still that stink of urine.

We crossed Rue de Dunkerque. Traffic in front of the station was still fairly heavy at that hour, and all the cafés were lit.

"Do you live around here?" I asked Charell.

"Not exactly . . . I'll explain."

At the corner of Rue de Compiègne, he pressed his forehead against the window of a large, empty café that was less brightly lit than the others. He seemed to be looking for someone. But there was no one in the main room, which was bathed in pale green light. Again he took my arm and we headed toward Boulevard Magenta.

"I have a little pied-à-terre here . . . For me and my wife . . . I'll explain."

We were at the foot of a dirty tan building that was very tall and shaped like the prow of a ship, the kind they used to build just before the war. An entrance door with frosted glass. To the left, a movie theater. They were showing several features, one of them titled *Asses High*.

A dozen men spewed from the theater just as we were about to enter the building: large dark suits, black briefcases, crewcuts. They bumped into me. One of them even trod on my foot, with his heavy shoe and reinforced sole. They followed their path in a straight line, unruffled, no doubt in search of a brasserie where they could wolf down a sauerkraut-and-sausage or fish stew before catching the northbound train.

"Strange neighborhood," I said to Charell as the elevator rose slowly in the dark, projecting the shadow of its grate on the wall at every landing.

The outside of the apartment door was reinforced with a rust-pocked armor plate. Charell stood aside to let me pass. We crossed through a foyer with red velvet walls, on which sconces with crystal pendants gave off a blinding light. The carpet was the same red as the velvet.

"This way, old man . . ."

A room with blank walls, its parquet floor gleaming under the ceiling fixtures. No furniture, save a wide leather couch on which a black girl of about twenty was asleep, wrapped in a plaid blanket. One of the two windows was open and looked out onto the narrow alley between the buildings.

"Have a seat, old man. Don't worry . . . when that one's asleep, she's dead to the world."

He pulled the window shut. We sat at the end of the couch. She was sleeping, her head thrown back slightly, neck arched. On the floor, a dog of impressive size, with long, curly black fur, was also asleep.

"She's pretty, don't you think?" Charell said, nodding at the girl. "I picked her up one evening on Rue de Maubeuge . . ."

Yes. She had a sweet, childlike face and a delicate neck.

"One of the reasons I rent this pied-à-terre," Charell said pensively, "is that I'd rather bring girls here than to our apartment in Neuilly. There was one once who made off with my wife's entire wardrobe."

I waited for him to offer some explanation. The girl had turned over and muttered a few indistinct words in her sleep. I admired her neck.

"It's also handy having this place because I travel north a lot for business. I'll explain . . ."

But he never explained a thing. A woman's ringing laugh broke the silence that had fallen between us. A shrill laugh, coming from the next room. Then a man's voice. And the laugh gradually became huskier.

Someone banged against the door. The laughing stopped. Sounds of a struggle or chase. Charell didn't react and lit a cigarette. I heard the woman's laugh again. After a while, moans that stretched longer and longer.

"When I said I traveled north," Charell said in a toneless voice, "I meant Belgium . . . I've got someone there who looks after my affairs. You know my father was Belgian. So am I . . ."

He was evidently trying to distract me. The dog emitted a few yaps, like an echo of the prolonged whimpers behind the door.

"But . . . you don't really live here, do you?" I asked.

"No, my wife and I live in Neuilly. Rue de la Ferme. Right

near where my parents lived . . . You remember what Rue de la Ferme was like."

"Yes."

"They tore down all the riding stables on the street . . ."

He suddenly looked devastated.

"A lot of things have changed since Valvert, old man . . ."

"Have you been married long?"

"Ten years. Suzanne is a lovely woman, you'll see."

I didn't dare ask if she was the one moaning and grunting behind the door. The sounds increased, then died down. Silence. We heard only the regular breathing of the black girl next to us, and less and less frequent yaps from the dog.

The door opened and a man appeared, in a light-colored checked jacket, a huge signet ring on his right hand. Blond, tall, stocky, with a mustache.

"This is François Duveltz, a friend," Charell said to me.

"I didn't know you were here," the other man said.

He lit a cigarillo. I felt embarrassed and kept my eyes fixed on his signet ring and sausagelike fingers. He walked to the window overlooking the alley and planted himself in front of the black, opaque glass that reflected the ceiling lights. There, at a slight distance, the window served as his mirror. He slowly straightened his tie.

"What are you up to, Alain? Are you staying over?"

"Yes, I'm staying over," Charell said curtly.

"I think I'll go take a spin around the neighborhood to see if there's any game . . ."

What sort of game was he talking about? What kind of strange hunt could one indulge in around the Gare du Nord?

"You want me to bring you back some game, Alain?"

He smiled, framed by the door to the foyer.

"No, thanks, not tonight," said Charell.

Still smiling, the other man gave us a wave of his right hand, the one with the signet ring, and disappeared.

The entry door slammed.

"He's an odd duck," said Charell. "I'll explain about him . . . Would you like some coffee?"

"No, thank you."

"Yes, yes, a drop of coffee. It'll do us all good . . . Just give me a moment—I'm going to run a bath for my wife . . ."

He went into the next room, leaving the door ajar. The black girl turned onto her left side, her head tilted and her cheek flattened against the edge of the couch. Soon I heard water running in a bathtub.

I stood up and went to the window. Human forms were staggering out of a bar. Soldiers on leave? Others were rushing, suitcase in hand, nearly getting themselves flattened by the cars and taxis screeching to a halt in front of the station. What kind of game could that guy have been talking about?

Over there, in the urine-smelling alley where Charell and I had emerged when we left the station, the girls were still standing by the fence, like lookouts. The white stain of a jacket, perhaps Duveltz's.

"Can you turn off the bath, Alain?" a woman said from the next room.

Charell's wife? He hadn't heard and the water continued to run. I felt like leaving the place, quietly, but that wouldn't have been nice to Alain.

I sat down again on the couch. The black girl stirred in her sleep and rested her bare foot against my knee. A chunky bracelet circled her ankle. The dog had awoken and clumsily padded up to me.

■

"You see how Rue de la Ferme has changed?" Charell said to me. "My parents' house is gone. So are the riding stables. Are you cold, darling? If you like, we can go back inside . . ."

He took off his jacket and draped it delicately over his wife's shoulders. We had just finished dining on the balcony of their apartment in Neuilly, on Rue de la Ferme.

Suzanne Charell had brown hair and blue eyes. Right away I liked the gentleness of her face, her cheekbones, her graceful bearing, and her straightforward manner. Alain had told me she often went riding, and that had won me over completely: I've always had a soft spot for women who go in for that sport.

And I was in fact thinking about horses as Suzanne served coffee and evening fell, a rather mild evening for early October. In the days of Valvert, on our Saturdays out, Alain would invite me to his house. I got off the metro at Pont de Neuilly, then followed Rue de Longchamp to Rue de la Ferme. Charell's parents lived in a townhouse, a kind of Trianon, framed by a close-cropped lawn like a velvet jewel case. Alain would take me across the street for a riding lesson. We were friends with the instructor's son, and we helped the boy and his father inspect the horses one last time before dinner—they called it the evening stable check. On Sunday mornings, very early, we rode on the street down to the Seine. The banks and the Ile de Puteaux were smothered in blue fog. Along the quays, white barriers and spiral staircases beneath the branches provided access to the barges, schooners, and small cargo vessels moored there in perpetuity, serving as houseboats.

"Have you known Alain a long time?" Suzanne asked.

"It's going on twenty years, eh, Patrick . . . ?"

We had met in the school infirmary, where we'd been admitted for the flu. The windows of our room looked out on the Bièvre, and at night we heard the murmur of the waterfalls. The nurse's name was Meg. She checked on us in the afternoon. We both had a crush on her and wanted to stay in that room as long as possible. Meg had served in the Indochina War and been one of the few women, along with Geneviève Vaudoyer, to jump with a parachute.

"Do you still know how to work a movie projector?" Charell asked me.

After Daniel Desoto was expelled, I had gotten Mr. Jeanschmidt to make Alain my co-projectionist. Twenty years already

. . . And yet, moments earlier, something from that time had still been floating in the air. Rue de Longchamp and Rue de la Ferme were deserted and silent. On the corner, a modern café had replaced the Lauby, with its mahogany paneling, but I wouldn't have been surprised to hear the fading clop of hooves and the murmur of leaves from the woods, to catch the scent of shadows and hay from the stables.

"What was Alain like twenty years ago?" Suzanne Charell asked with a smile.

"Very blond and skinny. We used to call him Aramis."

"This one here was Athos," said Charell. "The dreamer."

What had become of his parents? His father, with his saffron-yellow hair and mustache, looked like a major in the Indian Colonial forces. Had they disappeared, like their lawn and their Trianon? I didn't dare ask.

"Hey, do you remember when my father took us to the Comédie Française to see *Madame Sans-Gêne?*" Alain said.

Suzanne Charell had lit a cigarette and was looking steadily at me.

"Do you still ride, Suzanne?" I said to break the silence.

"Not much anymore."

"You know, Suzanne is a neighborhood girl . . . She grew up right near here, on Rue Saint-James."

"I might even have seen you, twenty years ago," said Suzanne. "But you wouldn't have noticed me. I was too little . . . I'm six years younger than Alain . . ."

"We might have passed Suzanne in the street, back in the day," I said.

Charell burst out laughing.

"And what would the three of us have done, eh?"

"I would have invited you to play hopscotch with me," said Suzanne.

They had moved nearer each other, and in their eyes I read their liking for me, but also a kind of helplessness, an unease, as if they were seeking the words to ask for my help or confess something.

■

That summery night, I had decided to return home from the Charells' on foot. I walked at random, sorry that I hadn't asked Alain more questions, but a kind of torpor had come over me: the entire evening I'd spent with them in the twilight of the balcony had a dreamlike haziness. And again, down the empty streets of Neuilly, I thought I heard the clop of horses' hooves and the rustle of leaves from twenty years ago. Stables . . .

I had reached the corner of Boulevard Richard-Wallace, in front of that curious Renaissance construction called the Château de Madrid. A black automobile pulled up beside me:

"Patrick . . ."

Alain Charell poked his head through the lowered window. He hadn't shut off the engine.

"Patrick, will you come with us to the Gare du Nord?"

Sitting next to him, Suzanne stared at me strangely, as if she didn't know me.

"Come with us to the Gare du Nord!"

His pupils were dilated. The two of them were frightening to look at.

"You know I can't. I have to go home . . ."

"You really can't come with us?"

"Another time."

"All right. Another time, then."

He had said it curtly, bobbing his head like a disappointed child who has been refused a sweet. He hit the gas and the car sped down Avenue du Commandant-Charcot. I started walking again. A few moments later, my heart leaped. The car had stopped about fifty yards ahead and its black coachwork gleamed in the moonlight. Charell got out, leaving the door open. He walked toward me.

"You *really* can't come to our place at Gare du Nord? I'd be so happy if you did . . . Suzanne, too . . . She really likes you . . ."

His lips sketched a smile.

"We'd feel a little less alone—you know?"

He shoved his hands into the pockets of his jacket, just as he used to shove them into the pockets of his blazer back in school. When he did, Mr. Lafaure, our chemistry teacher, would scold him for "hunching his back."

"But, Aramis, what goes on in that place, anyway?"

I tried to adopt a jocular tone.

"We . . . get together with friends . . . If you can call them friends . . . You get caught up . . . I'll explain . . ."

He smiled. He gave me a big thump on the shoulder.

"Obviously, it's not the same ambiance as the riding stables on Rue de la Ferme . . . Those were good times, eh, old man? . . . Phone me sometime . . ."

He returned with nervous steps to the car. The door slammed. He waved good-bye through the lowered window. And I, standing on the sidewalk, felt that I hadn't been very kind to my childhood friend. After all, if it meant so much to them, why *not* go with him and his wife to the Gare du Nord?

■

One night at around eleven o'clock, I was awoken by the ringing telephone.

"Patrick? It's Alain. Am I bothering you?"

"No, no, no bother," I said in a pasty voice.

"Could you come meet Suzanne and me? It's really important . . . We need to see you."

"Where are you?"

"At Gare du Nord."

"Gare du Nord?"

I felt devoid of will, about to be swept up by the tide, as in a bad dream. And maybe it *was* just a bad dream.

"So, are you coming?"

"Yes, I'm coming."

"Thank you, Patrick. We're on Rue de Dunkerque, in front of the station. In a brasserie next to the Terminus-Nord hotel. Did you get that?"

"Yes."

"It's called 'A l'Espérance.' Did you get that?"

"Yes."

"Come right away. It's urgent."

He had said it in a whisper, just before hanging up.

I went inside. The white light hurt my eyes and I felt stifled seeing all those people eating there, squeezed in by tens, twenties, as if around a communal or banquet table. The waiters zigzagged in the narrow gaps between tables, and an accordion player, perhaps there by mistake, mechanically fingered his instrument, its music smothered by the clamor of shouts and orders that rose and subsided. I navigated my way through the tables, peering at the scarlet faces of the diners, most of whom were shucking shellfish, white napkins tied around their necks.

Suzanne and Alain were sitting at the end of a long, empty table, in a corner at the back of the room. The numerous dishes had not been cleared away. I sat down next to Alain, facing Suzanne. She was wearing a man's raincoat that was too big for her, its collar up.

"Thanks for coming, old man."

He put his arm around my shoulder and leaned on me.

Suzanne raised her empty eyes to me, and I was alarmed by the pallor of her face. Was it the light that made her look so pale, or, by contrast, the black leatherette of the bench?

"What do you think of this place?" Charell asked in a falsely jovial voice. "One of the last authentic Parisian brasseries."

I had to lean closer to hear his voice. It was as if all those people talking too loudly around us were celebrating a wedding.

"Something to eat?"

I had set down next to me the present I'd wanted to give Suzanne Charell for the past several days, a handsome volume about equestrian sports that I'd found at a bookstore on Rue de Castiglione. But the gift struck me as ludicrous here in the back of this brasserie, before Suzanne's strained, white face.

She gripped my wrist and squeezed it hard.

"Please forgive me . . . I'm not feeling well . . . Not well at all . . ."

"Are you feeling ill, darling?" asked Charell.

She was deathly pale. Her head dropped like a stuffed doll's and she instinctively threw her arm forward to cushion her forehead.

"Don't worry, old man," Charell said to me. "It's going to be okay."

He lifted Suzanne by the shoulders and pulled her toward the door of the toilets. I followed them with my eyes. They walked slowly, her arm clinging to Alain's neck so as not to fall, raincoat floating about her like an old dressing gown. The noise in the room swelled. At one of the next tables, someone, a man with close-cropped hair, stood and proposed a toast, his forehead lathered in sweat. I looked down. Our tablecloth was spattered with wine stains, remnants of the diners who had been there before us, and the plate in front of me still held leftovers of head cheese.

Suzanne and Alain returned. He was holding her around the waist and she was walking more steadily. They sat down. Suzanne's face had regained some of its color but her pupils were strangely dilated. Alain's as well. She smiled beatifically.

"That's much better, isn't it, Suzanne?" said Charell.

"Oh, yes . . . So much better . . ."

"What if we go back to the apartment? Will you come with us, Patrick?"

Once outside, Charell proposed that we walk around the block. It had rained and the air was warm. Suzanne walked between us, holding each of us tightly by the arm.

We turned onto Boulevard Denain, a calm, tree-lined artery that avoided the agitation and tumult around the station. An empty bus was standing waiting, its driver having fallen asleep at the wheel. Hawaiian guitar music wafted from the entrance to a movie theater beneath the portico of a building.

We sat down on a bench. I held the book out to Suzanne.

"Here, this is for you."

She looked at me with her dilated pupils, holding shut the collar of her raincoat. She was shivering.

"Thank you . . . Thank you very much . . . That's so thoughtful of you . . ."

She laid the book on her knees.

She turned the pages and the three of us looked at the illustrations in the dim light. Suzanne and Alain still had that strange smile on their lips. They seemed lost in a dream.

After a while, Suzanne rested her head on my shoulder. They surely didn't want me to leave, and I suddenly thought we might spend the entire night on this bench. On the other side of the empty street, from a tarpaulin-covered truck with its lights out, two men in black leather jackets were unloading sacks of coal with rapid, furtive movements, as if on the sly.

■

Sometime later, a small notice in one of the evening papers:

Last night, an industrialist from Neuilly, Alain Charell, 36, was wounded by two gunshots in a furnished apartment at 126 Boulevard Magenta, where he was with his wife and several friends. According to witnesses, the shooting was accidental. The victim was taken to Hôtel-Dieu hospital.

They asked me to wait in a hallway with pale green walls, at the end of which was Charell's room.

The door opened. It wasn't the nurse but the black girl, the one who'd been sleeping on the couch the first time Alain had taken me to the apartment on Boulevard Magenta. She was wearing an elegant fitted suit, and I couldn't help thinking it belonged to Suzanne.

She sat down next to me and handed me an envelope.

"Alain asked me to give you this . . . He can't see you today . . . He's very tired."

I opened the envelope and read:

My dear Athos,

I have nothing to do in here but think about the days when things were better for us, when we were both in the school infirmary, getting the royal treatment from lovely Meg . . .

What a strange slope it's been these past twenty years, that has gradually led me from that infirmary to this hospital.

I'll explain.

Yours,

Aramis.

We walked out of the hospital, the black girl and I. She had tethered the huge dog with curly fur to a shrub. I helped her untie the leash.

"Is this your dog?"

"No. It belongs to Alain and Suzanne, but I'm looking after it."

She smiled at me.

"What happened?" I asked her.

She seemed reluctant to answer.

"It was bound to happen . . . They'll let just anybody into that apartment."

She shrugged. She didn't want to say any more.

"Have you known them long?" I asked.

"No, not very long . . . They're doing me a favor . . . Letting me stay at their place."

Perhaps she didn't trust me. After those gunshots, there would surely be an inquest.

"And what about you, have you known them long?"

"Alain is a childhood friend."

The dog walked about ten yards ahead of us, looking back now and again to verify we were still there. We had stopped talking, just walked beside each other. Yes, that tweed suit she was wearing was the one I'd seen on Suzanne Charell.

As we came to the Porte Saint-Denis, I suddenly realized that the huge, curly-haired dog would guide us, with its heavy, indolent step, all the way to the Gare du Nord.

XII.

Why did Marc Newman and I go so often to lay a flower on Oberkampf's tomb?

Behind the bunker rose an old wall, sheltered by clumps of rhododendrons. Newman scaled it first and dropped to the ground. Then he helped me climb down, supporting me by the waist. The enclosure was on lower ground, and the same wall, on the other side, was more than two yards high, and perfectly smooth.

It was like climbing down to the bottom of a well. It was cool on hot days, in that little garden where Oberkampf took his final repose. The bunker's shadow extended over the clumps of rhododendrons and the wall. Lower down, the leaves of a weeping willow half-concealed the tomb of Oberkampf, whose very name suggested water from a well, or black marble shimmering in the moonlight.

Newman had discovered this secret cloister, and we didn't dare ask Pedro whether it belonged to the Valvert estate; each time we ventured out, we never knew whether we'd have the strength to scale the wall in the opposite direction.

Newman lifted me onto his shoulders and I sat straddling the wall. I tugged Marc toward me with all my might. With an acrobatic pull-up, he vaulted fluidly over the wall. The momentum nearly made me topple over and break my neck.

Returning from Oberkampf's tomb, we were like two deep-sea divers, dazed to find ourselves back on the surface.

On summer nights, from our room in the Green Pavilion, we crept into the Swiss Yard, which we had to skirt as quickly as possible. We risked bumping into Pedro as he made his rounds, or Kovnovitsyn walking his dog Shoura. And we would have been grounded for going outside after curfew.

Once past the great lawn, we were safe. We plunged into the darkness of the park near the fitness trail and tennis courts. A path led up to the woods, and there we scaled the school's surrounding wall. We crossed through a clearing, at the end of which shone a vague dawn light, and finally reached the edge of the airfield that Newman had spotted one day, as he was walking near there.

Was this connected to the Villacoublay aerodrome? Newman claimed it wasn't. He had managed to get hold of a geological survey map, and we pored over it in minute detail: the airfield was nowhere to be found. We had marked its location with a cross, right in the middle of the woods.

We lay down on the grass, near the barbed-wire fence. Beyond it, shadowy figures entered the hangar, and when they came back out they were pushing carts or carrying suitcases. A car or truck stood waiting at the other end of the field, into which they loaded all these items. Soon, the sound of the engine faded away. There was a light outside the hangar, and at its entrance a few individuals in mechanics' overalls were playing cards around a table, or just eating. The murmur of their conversations in the night. Music. A woman's laughter. And often, they placed signals along the runway, as if to guide the landing of an airplane that never came.

"We'll have to find out what they're up to by day," Newman had said.

But by day, everything was empty and abandoned. Weeds had taken over the runway. In the back of the hangar, whose loose sheet metal rattled in the wind, slept the carcass of an old Farman biplane.

XIII.

Well, as it happens, I saw Newman again. A light green rubber ball had bounced off my shoulder. I turned around. A blonde little girl of about ten was looking at me shyly, hesitating to come retrieve her ball. Finally, she made up her mind. The ball had rolled on the sand a few yards away from me and, as if afraid I'd take it away, she grabbed it up quickly, crushed it against her chest, and ran.

That early afternoon, there were still very few of us on the beach. The little girl sat down, out of breath, next to a man in a navy blue swimsuit who was sunbathing, lying on his stomach, chin resting on his two fists. Given his close-cropped hair and very tanned—almost black—skin, it took me a moment to recognize my old schoolmate from Valvert, Marc Newman.

He smiled at me. Then he stood up. At fifteen, Newman, along with McFowles, had been one of the school's best field hockey players. He stopped in front of me, looking bashful.

The little girl, ball against her chest, had taken his hand and was eyeing me suspiciously.

"Edmond . . . Is that you?"

"Newman!"

He burst out laughing and gave me a hug.

"How about that! What are you doing here?"

"And you?"

"Me? I'm looking after the little one here . . ."

She now seemed completely reassured and gave me a smile.

"Corinne, this is an old friend of mine . . . Edmond Claude."

I held my hand out to her, and she, a bit hesitantly, held hers out to me.

"That's a very nice ball you've got," I said.

She tilted her head gently, and I was struck by how graceful she was.

"Are you on vacation?" Newman asked.

"No . . . I'm performing at the theater this evening. I'm on tour . . ."

"You became an actor?"

"Sort of," I said, feeling awkward.

"Are you sticking around for a while?"

"Unfortunately, no. I have to leave the day after tomorrow, with the tour."

"Oh, too bad."

He looked disappointed. He rested his hand on the little girl's shoulder.

"What about you—are you staying here long?" I asked.

"Oh, sure . . . Maybe for good," said Newman.

"For good?"

He seemed reluctant to talk in front of the child.

"Corinne, go put on your dress," said Newman.

Once the girl was out of earshot, Newman moved closer to me.

"Here's the thing," he said under his breath, "my name isn't Newman but Valvert . . . Valvert, like the school. I'm engaged to the girl's mother . . . We live in a villa, me, my fiancée, the little girl, my fiancée's mother, and this old guy who's my fiancée's mother's father-in-law. It might sound a bit complicated . . ."

He spoke breathlessly.

"A very respectable Nantes family. For me, you understand, it represents stability. No need to tell you that before this, I'd been pretty much adrift . . ."

The little girl walked toward us wearing a red dress with flounces. She had put her ball in a fishnet bag. With every step, she shook her foot, and sand poured from her sandals.

"I've knocked around all over the place," Newman whispered to me, with increasing urgency. "I even spent three years in the Foreign Legion . . . I'll tell you about it if we have time . . . But don't forget—Valvert . . . Don't mess up."

He pulled on a pair of sky-blue cotton trousers and a white cashmere sweater with the same suppleness as at school. I still recalled our wonder, and Kovnovitsyn's, at watching Newman turn cartwheels or climb a rope in mere seconds, legs thrust perpendicularly from his torso.

"You haven't changed," I said.

"Neither have you."

He grabbed the girl with both hands and, with an elegant

bend of his arms, sat her astride his shoulders. She laughed and rested the ball on Newman's skull.

"No galloping this time, Corinne. We're going back at a trot."

We headed toward the casino terrace.

"Let's go get something to drink," said Newman.

A tea room occupied the left wing of the casino, along with several shops. We sat at one of the outdoor tables, the space lined with tubs of red flowers. Newman ordered an espresso, as did I. The girl wanted ice cream.

"That's not very sensible, Corinne . . ."

She hung her head, disappointed.

"All right, fine, you can have ice cream . . . But you have to promise no more sweets this afternoon."

"I promise."

"You swear?"

She raised her arm to swear, and the ball she was holding against her chest fell to the ground. I picked it up and placed it gently on her knees.

The little girl ate her ice cream in silence.

Newman had opened the umbrella set in the middle of the table to give us some shade.

"So, you became an actor, just like that . . . ?"

"Afraid so, old man."

"You were in something at school . . . I remember it . . . What was that play again?"

"*Noah* by André Obey. I played Noah's daughter-in-law."

Newman and I both burst out laughing. The little girl raised her head and started laughing as well, not knowing why. Yes, I had enjoyed a certain success in that role, thanks to my bodice and peasant skirt.

"I would have loved to see you onstage tonight," said Newman. "But we're staying in at the villa. It's the old guy's birthday . . ."

"No matter. I've only got a bit part, you know."

In front of us, at the edge of the casino terrace, a poster for our play was affixed to a white pole that stood out against the blue sky like a ship's mast.

"Is that your show?" asked Newman.

"Yes."

The red letters of the title, *Mademoiselle Moi*, looked gay and summery, in harmony with the sky, the beach, and the rows of tents in the sunlight. From our seats, we could read the name of our lead actor and, with a bit more effort, that of my old friend Sylvestre-Bel, in letters half as large. But my name at the bottom of the poster wasn't visible. Short of using binoculars.

"So what about you, are you planning on settling here?" I asked Newman.

"Yes. I'm going to get married and try to start a business somewhere in the area."

"What kind of business?"

"A real estate agency."

The little girl finished her ice cream and Newman distractedly stroked her blond hair.

"My wife-to-be wants to stay here. Partly because of Corinne.

It's better for a child to grow up near the ocean than in Paris . . . You should see her school. It's a few miles from here, in a chateau with a park. And guess who used to own the chateau? Winegrain, one of the kids from Valvert."

I hadn't really known Winegrain, but his name at school was legendary, along with a few others: Yotlande, Bourdon . . .

"Our villa is behind the casino. On the main road. I would have invited you over for a drink this evening, but the old coot is always in such a crappy mood . . ."

He had stretched his legs out on a chair and folded his arms, with the same air of an athlete at rest as he used to have during recess.

"So why did you change your name?" I asked in a low voice, after the girl had left the table.

"Because I'm starting over from scratch."

"Still, if you want to get married, you'll have to give your real name."

"Not true. I'll have new ID papers . . . Nothing to it, old man."

He shook each foot and his white espadrilles fell off one after the other.

"What about the kid? Does she have a father?"

She was looking in the window of a hairdresser's shop a bit farther on, very stiff and serious, the ball between her stomach and crossed hands.

"No, no . . . Her father bailed. No one knows where he is . . . Besides, so much the better . . . I'm her father now."

I didn't dare ask any more questions. Already in school, Newman shrouded himself in mystery, and whenever we tried to find out more about him—his address, his exact age, his nationality—he smiled without answering, or changed the subject. And whenever a teacher called on him in class, he would immediately stiffen and keep his lips sealed. We had ended up writing off his attitude as pathological shyness, and the teachers stopped calling on him, which absolved him from having to study.

I plucked up my courage.

"What have you been doing up to now?"

"Everything," Newman answered with a sigh. "I spent three years in Dakar working in an import-export firm. Two years in California, where I opened a French restaurant . . . Before either of those, I did my military service in Tahiti . . . I stayed there quite a while . . . I ran into one of our classmates on Moorea . . . Portier . . . You know—Christian Portier . . ."

He spoke quickly, feverishly, as if he hadn't opened up to anyone in a long time and was afraid some intruder would interrupt him before he had a chance to finish.

"Meanwhile, I enlisted in the Legion. I was there for three years. Then I deserted . . ."

"You deserted?"

"Well, not really . . . I managed to get hold of some medical certificates. I was wounded over there, and I could even claim an invalid's pension . . . After that, I worked for a while as Mme Fath's chauffeur."

Despite his candid, athletic demeanor, a kind of fog enveloped the young man. Everything about him, apart from his sporting abilities, was vague and indistinct. Back then, in school, an old gentleman used to come collect him on our Saturdays out, or visit him during the week. He had skin like porcelain, a cane, shallow-set eyes, and he leaned his delicate frame on Newman's arm. Marc had introduced him to me as his father.

He wore a flannel suit with a silk pocket square. He had an unplaceable accent. And Newman indeed called him Dad. But one afternoon, our teacher had announced to Newman that "Mr. Condriatseff was waiting for him on the patio." It was the old man. Newman would write to him, and the name on the envelope intrigued me: Condriatseff. I had asked about it, but he merely smiled . . .

"It would be great if you could be best man at my wedding," said Newman.

"When is it?"

"End of the year. To give us time to find an apartment in the area. We can't keep living at the villa with the old guy and my wife-to-be's mother. Personally, I'd love to have a place in there."

With a nonchalant wave, he indicated the large, modern apartment buildings at the end of the bay.

"What about your wife-to-be, where did you meet her?"

"In Paris . . . When I got out of the Foreign Legion. Needless to say, I wasn't in great shape. She really helped me out . . . You'll see, she's a great girl . . . At the time, I couldn't even cross the street by myself . . ."

He seemed to be taking his new paternal responsibilities seriously and didn't let the little girl out of his sight. She was still absorbed in contemplating the storefront windows of the casino.

He leaned his head toward me and jerked his chin toward the street that ran alongside the casino and down to the beach.

"Look," he said under his breath. "It's my fiancée and her mother..."

Two dark-haired women of the same height. The younger of the two had long hair and was wearing a terrycloth robe that reached halfway down her thighs. The other had on a sarong in rust and pastel-blue tones. They glided by a few feet away, but didn't see us behind the tubs of flowers and bushes.

"It's funny," Newman said. "From a distance, they both look the same age... They're pretty, don't you think?"

I admired their lissome gait, their posture, their long, tanned legs. They stopped at the empty embankment, took off their high heels, and slowly descended the steps to the beach, as if offering themselves to everyone's gaze as long as possible.

"I sometimes get the two of them confused," Newman said dreamily.

They had left something mysterious in their wake. Airwaves. Under their spell, I scanned the beach, hoping to spot them again.

"Later on, I'll introduce you... You'll see. The mother's just as attractive as the daughter. They have these great cheekbones and violet eyes. *My* problem is that I love them both the same."

The little girl returned to our table at a run.

"Where have you been?" said Newman.

"I went to look at all the *Applekins* books in the bookstore."

She was out of breath. Newman took the ball from her hands.

"Soon it'll be time to go back to the beach," he said.

"Not right away," the little girl said.

And, moving closer to Newman:

"Gérard, will you buy me an *Applekins?*"

Gérard?

She lowered her head shyly, blushing at having dared ask for the book.

"Okay . . . All right . . . Just as long as you don't eat any sweets this afternoon . . . Actually, why don't you get three of them . . . You never know, we should stock up for later."

He dug in his pocket, pulled out a crumpled banknote, and handed it to her.

"And pick me up the latest issue of *Pleasures of France.*"

"Three *Applekins?*" the girl asked, wide-eyed.

"Yes, three . . ."

"Oh, thank you, Gérard!"

She threw herself into his arms and kissed him on both cheeks. Then she ran off across the casino terrace.

"You're calling yourself Gérard these days?" I asked.

"Sure. If you're changing your name, might as well go for broke."

On the avenue, to our right, a man appeared, with a ruddy complexion and a gray crewcut. He walked with quick, regular steps, wearing a brown smoking jacket, blue pants, and carpet slippers.

"Hey, there's the geezer," said Newman. "He's spying on us. Every afternoon, he makes sure we're really at the beach. He's a tough old bird for seventy-three, take my word for it . . ."

The man was tall and held himself very erect. His bearing suggested something military. He sat down on a bench on the embankment, facing the shore.

"He's keeping an eye on Françoise and her mother," Newman said. "You have no idea what it's like to turn around and find his prison guard face staring at you . . ."

Apparently it gave him the shivers. A short distance away, the old man stood up now and again, leaned his elbows on the embankment railing for a while, then went back to his bench.

"He's a real son of a bitch. Françoise's mother has to put up with him because he's supporting them—her, Françoise, and the kid. Bitter old coot. On top of which, he added a 'de' to his name, so now he calls himself 'Grout de l'Ain,' but he used to be in real estate. You can't imagine how tightfisted the guy is. Françoise's mother has to keep accounts and jot down every paper clip she buys . . . He's completely ostracized *me*—he pretends I'm not even there. He won't let me sleep in the same room as Françoise. Right off the bat, he's been suspicious of me because of this . . . Look . . ."

He yanked up the left sleeve of his sweater, uncovering a compass rose tattooed on his forearm.

"You see . . . And yet it's hardly anything bad."

"You should get married as soon as you can and go live somewhere else," I said.

Over there, on his bench, the old man had meticulously unfolded a newspaper.

"Edmond . . . Can I tell you something in confidence?"

"Of course."

"Listen . . . They want me to do away with Grout de l'Ain."

"Who does?"

"Françoise and her mother. They want me to get rid of the old coot."

His features were tense and a large horizontal wrinkle cut across his forehead.

"The problem is how to do it cleanly, so as not to rouse any suspicion . . ."

The blue sky, the beach, the orange-and-white-striped tents, the tubs of flowers in front of the casino, and that old man, over there on his bench, reading his newspaper in the sun . . .

"Try as I might, I can't think of a good way to get rid of him. I've made two attempts. First with my car. One night, he was taking a walk outside and I nearly ran him over . . . like an accident . . . It was idiotic."

He was watching for a reaction from me, an opinion. I nodded inanely.

"The second time, we were walking on the boulders around Batz-sur-Mer, a few miles from here. I was going to push him off . . . And then at the last minute I lost my nerve. What do you make of all this?"

"I don't quite know what to say," I told him.

"Anyway, I wouldn't be taking much of a risk. I'll have Françoise and her mother's testimony to back me up. We often talk about it, the three of us. They think the best way would be to take him on another walk in Batz . . ."

My gaze rested on the old man a short distance away, who had refolded his newspaper and taken a pipe from his pocket, which he was filling slowly. What was his name, Grout de l'Ain? I felt like shouting it out to see if he'd look over. The little girl, her books under her arm, a radiant smile on her face, came back to sit at our table.

I was puzzled. That fog from fifteen years ago still clung to Marc Newman. His art of not answering precise questions. But I also remembered his sudden bouts of talkativeness, like jets of steam under a heavy lid. How could one ever know with him? Condriatseff.

Vague thoughts crossed my mind, on the sidewalk of that café, in the sun, while a breeze swelled the orange-and-white-striped tents and ruffled our play poster on the ship's mast. I said to myself that our school had left us completely unprepared for life.

She was showing Newman the pictures in *Applekins*, and he, leaning over her shoulder, was turning the pages of the booklet. Now and again, she raised her face toward Marc and smiled. She seemed very fond of him.

XIV.

It's a night unlike any other. I caught the last train, the eleven-forty-three. Charell is waiting for me on the platform. We walk through the lobby with its closed ticket windows, then the traffic circle in front of the station, the one I used to ride around on a bike with Martine and Yvon.

We enter the street, taking the sidewalk that runs along the public park. On the other side, a warm breeze caresses the ivy at the Robin des Bois inn, its bar still lit at this late hour. Charell goes in to buy a pack of cigarettes. But no one is there.

We resume our walk. On the left, beneath the concrete balcony, the brown doors of the cinema with their portholes. An avenue bordered by linden trees rises toward Rue du Docteur-Dordaine, where Martine and Yvon lived. The bus stop. After so many years, Bordin's catchphrase comes to mind:

"A giovedí, amici miei . . ."

The railroad crossing. Town hall. And pensive Oberkampf in his bronze frock coat. He's the only resident left. We hear the flow of the Bièvre waterfall, under the bridge.

The main gate is left ajar. The driveway stretches before us, but we hesitate. Gradually, in that nocturnal northern light, appear the infirmary, the flagpole, and the trees.

The two of us enter. We don't dare venture farther than the large plane tree.

The grass glows with a pale green phosphorescence. It was there, at that spot on the lawn, that we waited for Pedro's whistle to start the match. We were such fine boys.

PATRICK MODIANO, winner of the 2014 Nobel Prize in Literature, was born in Boulogne-Billancourt, France, in 1945, and published his first novel, *La Place de l'Etoile*, in 1968. In 1978, he was awarded the Prix Goncourt for *Rue des Boutiques Obscures* (published in English as *Missing Person*), and in 1996 he received the Grand Prix National des Lettres for his body of work. Modiano's other writings in English translation include *Suspended Sentences*, *Pedigree: A Memoir*, *After the Circus*, *Paris Nocturne*, *Little Jewel*, and *Sundays in August* (all published by Yale University Press), as well as the memoir *Dora Bruder*, the screenplay *Lacombe Lucien*, and the novels *So You Don't Get Lost in the Neighborhood*, *Young Once*, *In the Café of Lost Youth*, and *The Black Notebook*.

MARK POLIZZOTTI has translated more than forty books from the French, including works by Gustave Flaubert, Patrick Modiano, Marguerite Duras, Jean Echenoz, and Raymond Roussel. A Chevalier of the Ordre des Arts et des Lettres and the recipient of a 2016 American Academy of Arts and Letters Award for Literature, he is the author of *Revolution of the Mind: The Life of André Breton*, which was a finalist for the PEN/Martha Albrand Award for First Nonfiction, the collaborative novel *S.*, *Luis Buñuel's Los Olvidados*, and *Bob Dylan: Highway 61 Revisited.* His essays and reviews have appeared in the *New Republic*, the *Wall Street Journal*, *ARTnews*, the *Nation*, *Parnassus*, *Partisan Review*, *Bookforum*, and elsewhere. He directs the publications program at The Metropolitan Museum of Art in New York.